THE WORLD WRECKER

The strange reports came from all over the world. Reports of a bearded man who could walk through solid walls. Business conferences found a stranger listening to their secret plans; military documents and gold reserves disappeared from impregnable safes; Miss World completely vanished from a locked room before the eyes of several astonished witnesses. Cities were destroyed by gigantic earthquakes; bridges and all metal structures simply dissolved ... in fact the people of the Earth faced complete and utter destruction!

SYDNEY J. BOUNDS

THE WORLD WRECKER

Complete and Unabridged

LINFORD
Leicester

First published in Great Britain

First Linford Edition
published 2009

British Library CIP Data

Bounds, Sydney J.
  The world wrecker.—Large print ed.—
Linford mystery library
  1. Suspense fiction
  2. Large type books
  I. Title
  823.9'12 [F]

  ISBN 978–1–84782–598–8

Published by
F. A. Thorpe (Publishing)
Anstey, Leicestershire

Set by Words & Graphics Ltd.
Anstey, Leicestershire
Printed and bound in Great Britain by
T. J. International Ltd., Padstow, Cornwall

This book is printed on acid-free paper

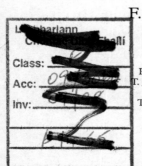

Prologue

He did not remember very much. The control rods had jammed, resulting in a catastrophic surge of power through the atomic pile. It did not explode in the sense that a bomb explodes; rather, it boiled over, melting away the protective walls to unleash vast quantities of deadly radiation.

Ralph Savage, atomic physicist, was alone with the pile when the disaster occurred. The clangour of a warning bell almost drowned the chatter of Geiger counters; the needle indicating the energy level of the plant soared past the red line marking the limit of safety.

There was nothing he could do. Already his body felt as if it were on fire. He must get away before it was too late — that was his last conscious thought before oblivion came. He knew nothing of the grim-faced men in protective clothing who dragged him clear of the pile with long-handled tongs.

For Ralph Savage, there were periods of intermittent consciousness when pain returned and he cried out for succour; periods of darkness alternating with a vague awareness of white uniforms and soft voices. A mist obscured the room.

Time passed, and it was as if he looked on from outside his own body, all feeling suspended; looked on as the hypodermic needle pierced his skin and orderlies wheeled him to the operating theatre. There were moments when he was aware of cool white walls and the tray of instruments beside his bed, the sympathetic smile of a night nurse.

It was months before he felt able to take an interest in his future . . . and then he was told the truth. He would live, but his life would hardly be worth the living. Science could not give him a new body and that was what he needed; his face was disfigured and even plastic and cosmetic surgery could do little for him. All he could look forward to was years in hospital, undergoing continuous treatment — and they hinted that they did not know all the effects radiation might have on him.

The outlook for Ralph Savage was dark indeed. He would be well cared for, they assured him; the government had allotted him a substantial pension. He would lack nothing . . . except health, his work, ambition. And Savage was ambitious, a man who had risen fast in his profession with a bright future before him.

All that was wiped out at a single stroke. Fate had dealt him a cruel blow. Fate — or society? Savage brooded on his misfortune while they injected him to drug the pain, peeled off dead skin and grafted on new. His brooding changed to hatred of the society that had done this thing to him, and his mind warped under the strain of accepting his deformation.

He became withdrawn. He would lie for hours in his bed, not speaking a word — a pale, tense figure with darkly-glittering eyes — planning the revenge he would one day take. The months passed and hatred grew within him like a cancer; there was the one thought in his head — society must be made to pay, and pay dearly, for what it had taken from him.

One night, under cover of darkness, he left his bed and dressed. In preparation for this moment he had secured a large sum of money in notes; he hired a car and drove off . . . and disappeared as completely as if the ground had opened to swallow him.

The car was found later, abandoned, and a search made, but no one ever found his trail. The hospital authorities shrugged and left it to the police, who consigned his name with thousands of others to their Missing Persons file. In time, even his colleagues at the atomic power station ceased to wonder what had happened to him.

Years afterwards, a gaunt, heavily-bearded figure moved through the heart of the South American jungle. The Wild One, the Indians called him, and left him strictly alone.

Machete in hand, he penetrated the green wall of the tropics oblivious to heat and insects alike. He carved his own path while the parrots screeched and monkeys swung from lianas.

Gigantic trees thrust broad foliage up to the sky, patterning the undergrowth with gloomy shadows; a strange, phosphorescent light crept between their boles. He paddled against the current of backwater tributaries, striking ever deeper into the interior.

The cries of wild animals were the only voices he heard. A fugitive from civilization, he enjoyed this pagan paradise with its luxuriant and exotic beauty, its abundant and terrible life.

His clothes were in rags, his legs bare and scarred. When he was hungry he trapped small animals or plucked berries and fruits; he drank from the rivers. At night he would make a fire and sleep on the ground. During the rainy season he built a mud hut to shelter in; fever racked his body, but he survived. He wandered restlessly, always alone, driven by an urge that now bore little relation to his mode of living.

There came an evening when the rays of a setting sun threw bloody light over the jungle and revealed a vertical precipice that dropped sheer away at his feet. Looking down, he saw a small valley, remote and unsuspected, surrounded entirely by high cliffs. A broad river wound across the plain, which bore signs of cultivation, and beside a lake stood the ruins of an ancient temple. Beyond the temple, the sullen snout of a volcano poured forth dark smoke.

Something tall and slender jutted from the ground below — something that had the high polish of worked metal caught the sun's rays and flashed a challenge to him. He could not imagine what it was, but his curiosity was roused. Tomorrow he would descend to the valley and take a closer look.

That night he slept on the rim; and he slept but fitfully for the strangely slanting column of metal was somehow sinister, promising everything that his tortured mind desired. In his dreams he ravaged its secrets and became master of new and terrible weapons with which to wreak his vengeance.

Descending the precipice was not easy, but he managed it. He crossed the plain, heading towards that tantalizing gleam of metal. The Indians of the valley were unlike any other savages he had met in the jungle; taller and more regal of bearing, they wore short, white tunics of woven cloth and tilled the land. The carved stonework of the temple, with its boldly incised line and fantastic design, gave him a clue to their identity — he had stumbled upon descendants of the ancient Inca civilization.

He strode among them with the arrogance of a superior being, noting how they shrank from him. Perhaps it was because they had never seen a white man — or perhaps because of his cruelly mutilated face, only half-concealed by his beard. At all events, he had nothing to fear from them.

The column of metal turned out to be cylindrical, twenty yards across and a hundred and twenty yards high. The topmost point was rounded, almost like a bullet. Near the ground a circular port gave entrance to the construction; and the interior was filled by machines of alien design.

Ralph Savage laughed to himself and

his eyes glowed with a fanatical light. He had seen paintings of such things, by artists who drew on their imagination — now the reality was before him. His chance had come at last . . .

He had found a vessel that had crossed space from another world, and all the secrets of this other race were his to use for his own purposes.

1

The ghosts

Detective Inspector Arthur Crispian was a big man. Standing six-feet-one without his boots, broad of chest and bull-necked, his lower limbs were short enough to give him an appearance of top-heaviness. His arms were too long for his thickset body like those of a gorilla.

He dressed in a dark grey suit with a light blue tie, and looked as if a rugby player had been forced into the elegant suiting of a West-End tailor — the clothes had suffered in the process.

His features were rugged, not handsome, but interesting the way a Cornish cliff is interesting, hard and solid and full of character. His hair was a fiery red, untamed by the morning's struggle with brush and comb; and his eyes normally held a dreamy expression, indicating that here was that rare personality, a man of strong physique with powers of the imagination.

He was the only member of Scotland Yard to have run his own private detective agency.

Just now, he was seated at his desk and looking all the larger because of the smallness of his office. From the high window he had a view of the Thames Embankment; and the hooting of tugs merged with the roar of London's traffic. He had an official file open before him and was reading the topmost report, a frown on his face.

Across the desk, Detective Sergeant Bill Williams turned the pages of a popular film magazine. Williams was slimly-built, a head shorter than Crispian, with an aquiline nose and penetrating gaze. He had a debonair manner, which was seldom ruffled and followed the gossip pages relating to his favourite film stars with the avidity of a teenager.

'Nice looking girl,' he commented, holding up the magazine for Crispian to see. 'British, too. She ought to win easily, in my opinion, but I'll bet the contest is fixed. All these beauty competitions are the same — some Hollywood starlet will walk off with the first prize.'

Crispian looked at the picture. He saw an attractive young girl in a one-piece swimsuit; she was long-legged, with a graceful figure and light-coloured hair that descended in sleek waves about her shoulders. Her face was delicately formed and the eyes that smiled back at him were intelligent as well as beautiful. She certainly ought to stand a good chance of winning, Crispian thought . . .

The caption read:

Mary Marshall is the sole representative from Great Britain among the finalists in the World Beauty Contest, to be held in Los Angeles next month.

'She looks too well-bred for that sort of thing,' Crispian observed.

'Why shouldn't a smart girl cash in on her looks?' Williams demanded. 'She won a free passage to the States and stands to collect Big Bucks in prize money — besides the chance of breaking into films. That's better than being a police-woman!'

11

He studied the picture again and sighed.

'Wouldn't mind dating her myself . . . '

Crispian laughed.

'What a hope! Better forget her, Bill — she's in California and you're here. You've no more chance of meeting her than I have.'

It was a sore point with Inspector Crispian that the girls who attracted him were not interested in him.

'Put that paper away,' he grunted. 'We've work to do. You've read these reports — what do you make of them?'

'Cranks,' Williams said briefly. 'No one can walk through walls.'

Crispian frowned, moving papers to make a pattern on his desk.

'Nevertheless, there's something queer going on. If it was just one report I'd agree with you, but . . . listen to this:

''Statement by Miss P. Swayle of 153a Kensington Crescent. Yesterday evening at about half-past seven I decided to take a bath. I bolted the door on the inside and drew the curtains across the window. The bathroom is quite small and there was nowhere anyone could hide. I was sitting in the bath when, suddenly, a man appeared in the room. I screamed and grabbed a towel to cover myself. He was hideously ugly, the lower half of his face concealed by a thick beard, and wore a plain white tunic and sandals. I asked him how he'd got in and told him to leave, but he only laughed and stared at me with dark, glittering eyes. I was scared and pressed the bell-push to summon help. Then he moved back to the wall and walked through it. I am certain he did not use the door. I have never seen him before.'

'A constable investigated,' Crispian continued, turning a page. 'He found footprints on the damp floor and the window still fastened on the inside. He searched the building and vicinity without finding anyone answering to the description.'

'I'm not surprised,' Williams said. 'She imagined it — sounds like some dried-up old maid with men on the brain.'

'That doesn't fit the character of Miss Swayle given by other residents of 153a

Kensington Crescent,' Crispian remarked drily. 'I gather she isn't the sort of woman to lack male companionship. I just don't know what to make of it, unless she forgot to bolt the door after all.'

'That's the answer,' Williams returned confidently. 'You can bet on it!'

* * *

The chairman stood at one end of a long, polished table.

'Gentlemen,' he began, 'you already know why I have called this meeting. Our chief rivals, Commercial Plastics, are about to put a new polythene product on the market. I have been fortunate in acquiring an inside contact, and it appears that Commercial Plastics are sinking an enormous amount of capital into this venture.'

He paused, allowing himself a brief smile.

'Now we already have a similar process, and I am confident that we can manufacture at substantially less cost than our rivals. What I propose, therefore, is this: we will hold up distribution of our own product until after Commercial Plastics have put theirs on the market. By doing so, we shall ensure that they commit themselves fully — then we can push our own variation of the new plastic at a lower price, taking the market from them and going some way to put them out of business!

'Gentlemen, you will observe that this plan depends for its success on complete secrecy. No hint that we have a similar process must leave this room. Commercial Plastics must suspect nothing. The business of this meeting must be treated as highly confidential — '

The chairman's voice faded off as he realized that he no longer had the attention of his colleagues. They were staring behind him, their gaze transfixed. He looked quickly over his shoulder.

The stranger could not possibly have got into the room, but there he was; an ugly fellow in queer clothes. It was a shock. How much had he heard, the chairman wondered? Well, he couldn't be allowed to repeat the conversation . . .

'Hold him!' he shouted, and threw himself at the intruder.

He was not quick enough. The bearded man stepped back, his hands fumbling with some contraption belted to his waist — and the chairman struck blindly at the wall. The stranger vanished as mysteriously as he had come, vanished into the wall.

★　★　★

Sir Godfrey radiated good humour as he shook hands with the Soviet delegation. He escorted them to the door with cordialities on his lips and the secret resolve to recommend the new weapon, plans of which were in a wall safe in that very room. They would, he thought, have given a great deal to learn the contents of his safe.

Not that there was any chance of that. He alone knew the combination and the lock was of a type to defy even an expert cracksman. The plans were secure where he had put them twelve hours before.

As soon as the Russians were off the

premises, he returned to his office, locked the door and drew heavy curtains across the windows. He pressed the button that moved part of the wall, exposing the complicated mechanism of the safe. His fingers eagerly picked out the key symbols, completing the combination — and the door swung open at his touch.

The safe was not empty; but the plans had gone and in their place was a small heap of ashes.

Newspapers carried the stories almost daily:

THE GHOSTS AGAIN!
MAN WALKS THROUGH WALL OF NEWSPAPER OFFICE
STRANGE HAPPENINGS IN LOCKED ROOM

The reports were vague as to factual content and written in the most sensational style. Exactly who first labelled them 'The Ghosts' is not known, but the term was apt and caught the public's imagination. Who but a ghost could penetrate locked doors and solid walls?

Psychical societies claimed them as new evidence for life beyond the grave. Scientists frowned and talked of hallucination and mass-hysteria. A stream of indignant letters to Parliament complained that an Englishman's private life was no longer private.

Whatever the truth behind these reports in the national press, it could hardly be doubted that some strange phenomenon was involved — though exactly what, no one knew, for unprejudiced accounts were hard to come by. The shock of actually encountering a ghost too often rendered the observer incapable of giving a coherent account. Descriptions were usually vague and contradictory.

And not only Britain suffered from these visitations; Continental and American papers carried similar stories. It began to look as though no place on Earth was safe from the prying eyes of — The Ghosts!

★ ★ ★

Crispian came to the last report in his file.

'Statement by Toni Ley, chef at the *Jongleur Café*, Soho: On the fifth of the month, I prepared dinner for a select party. Soup had been served and the main course — duck with green peas and creamed potatoes — stood ready on a tray with a bottle of Chateau Neuf. The tray was on a table near the service door. I heard footsteps and turned round, expecting to see Albert, the waiter. Instead, I saw a bearded man with a deformed face. I asked him what he was doing in my kitchen and, when he picked up the tray, moved quickly to place myself between him and the door. He ignored me and walked through the wall opposite, carrying the tray. Later, I cooked a fresh dinner for my party.'

Crispian laid down the file, a half-smile on his lips.

'It would seem that even ghosts get hungry, Sergeant, and that indicates a material body — one we may get the chance to lay our hands on.'

'Maybe,' Williams grunted. 'I'm not convinced that anyone has walked through a wall. I'll believe that when I see it for myself.'

Crispian frowned.

'Nevertheless, there are too many reports — and they're too widespread — for us to ignore altogether. Reports from Berlin to Madrid, from Chicago to Cincinnati. And there's another point; no valuables have been taken . . . it's simply a question of some person or persons unknown prying into the private affairs of other people.'

Williams grinned, admiring the picture of Mary Marshall.

'I wouldn't mind taking a peek at her,' he said, 'but no such luck for a poor copper. Tell you what,' he added brightly, 'I'll bet it's an advertising stunt!'

'I don't know.' Crispian scratched at his mop of red hair. 'I don't know about that . . . the whole thing's crazy.'

'You can say that again.'

For some minutes neither man spoke. Crispian puzzled over the strange occurrences, while his sergeant returned to a study of Britain's last hope in the world beauty contest.

'I can't see what to do about it, anyway. Unless — '

The inter-office phone buzzed and Crispian picked up the receiver. As he listened, his eyes lost their dreamy look.

'Yes, sir. I understand, sir. I'll get over there right away.'

He replaced the phone and pushed back his chair in one movement.

'Bill, grab a car fast. Gold bullion has disappeared from the vaults below the Bank of England!'

2

Vanished gold

A crowd was already gathering as the police car pulled into the kerb in the shadow of that towering greystone building on Threadneedle Street. Reporters tried to question Crispian and Williams as they ran up the steps to the massive portal of the Bank.

'Like ruddy vultures,' Williams grumbled. 'The newspapers get on to anything like this as fast as we do. They're a damn nuisance!'

Crispian showed his identification to a uniformed constable at the door and the two detectives passed inside. There was an air of excitement in the building; small groups of clerks were talking animatedly and no business was being transacted. Nothing like this had happened before . . .

'The Bank Guard is still on duty,'

Crispian observed.

An official directed them to the Governor's office, a large oak-panelled room with thick pile carpets and leather-upholstered furniture. The Governor of the Bank of England was tall and immaculately dressed, his hair beginning to take on a silver sheen and a tiny furrow of worry between his eyes.

'Thank goodness you've arrived, Inspector! I really don't know what to do — the whole thing is quite incredible. Until this moment, I would have said it was impossible for anyone to remove bullion from our strongrooms. We have an elaborate system of safeguards.'

'Give me the facts,' Crispian returned briskly. 'Then I'll take a look at the vaults.'

'Only one vault has been entered, Inspector. It contained gold ingots to the value of a million pounds sterling — now it is empty. The gold was checked yesterday, in preparation for dispatch to the United States. Officially, no one has entered the vault and, even now, I do not see how anyone could. The doors are double-locked and a man posted on guard outside. There is an automatic warning system that operates if the locks are tampered with — needless to say, no warning was given. There is no other entry and the walls, roof and door are thick concrete. The air conditioning ducts are too small to admit a human being.'

'Who discovered the theft?' Williams asked.

'Mr. Beadnell, who is in charge of bullion here. An entirely reliable man — he has been with the Bank for nearly forty years. This is a terrible shock for him.'

'I'd like to question Beadnell,' Crispian said.

'Of course, Inspector. I anticipated that and asked him to wait in the next room.'

The Governor crossed to the connecting door and opened it.

'Come in, Mr. Beadnell. These gentlemen are from Scotland Yard.'

Crispian observed Beadnell closely; he saw a small man, dressed in sober black, his face grey and his hands betraying agitation.

'Will you tell me exactly what happened this morning?' the Inspector asked.

'Yes, sir. I went to Number Three vault to see about the dispatch of gold. I had a clerk with me, two men for handling the ingots, and two guards. I opened the vault — only the Governor and myself know the combination, which is changed regularly — and saw blank shelves. The bullion was no longer there! At first, I could hardly believe my eyes. No one could have got into the strongroom — certainly the gold could not be removed without my knowledge — yet the impossible had happened. I tell you, Inspector, it's fantastic . . . like black magic!'

Crispian grunted.

'We'll see about that. Cast your mind back to yesterday — you noticed nothing unusual then?'

'No, nothing at all.'

'All right,' Crispian decided, 'I'd like to see the vault now.'

He left the Governor's office with Beadnell and Sergeant Williams. A lift cage carried them below ground. At the bottom two guards checked their identity. They walked along a windowless passage to a metal door labelled: Vault Three. Beadnell opened it and the two police officers stepped inside.

The strongroom was a hollow cube of reinforced concrete, with steel shelves lining the walls. The shelves were empty.

'The alarm mechanism has not been tampered with?' Crispian asked.

'No, inspector — we had a man examine it immediately. He swears that no one could have opened the door without sounding the alarm.'

Crispian moved round the vault, testing the walls and the metal grille over the air duct. There was no sign of a forced entry.

'Looks like someone walked through the wall,' Williams said, with an attempt at humour.

Crispian worked methodically over the floor. Suddenly, he bent down and scooped up something green with his hand.

'What do you suppose this is, Sergeant?'

Williams stared blankly.

'Why, it's a piece of leaf. I wonder how that got here.'

'Crushed, as if someone walked on it and it stuck to his foot. Not a British plant, either — a tropical species, I'd say.' Crispian placed the fragment of bruised leaf in an envelope and turned to Beadnell. 'Do you know if anyone on your staff cultivates tropical plants?'

'Not as far as I know,' Beadnell answered.

Crispian took a final look round.

'All right, Williams, turn the lab boys loose. I want a complete report on anything they find — I'm going to Kew to see if the experts can identify this leaf. Meet me at the Yard when you're through.'

★ ★ ★

Some hours later, Crispian had the sum total of information. A few blurred fingerprints, not in the criminal records, and a cast of a print made by a man's sandal. The leaf, he learned, came from a plant common to South America.

Routine questioning of the Bank Guard revealed nothing. A late-night reveller had come forward; he stated that he had been in the vicinity of the Bank and had seen a queerly dressed man vanish through a stone wall. The sight had sobered him up quickly.

And that was all . . . of the missing gold, there was no trace.

Crispian sighed unhappily. It began to look as if someone really could walk through walls and, if so, he had a feeling this wasn't going to be the last mysterious robbery. He didn't like to think what the newspapers and broadcasting media would make of it . . .

★　★　★

The Commissioner frowned and pushed Crispian's report aside.

'It's a damn queer business, Inspector, but we can't leave it at that. The papers are kicking up hell. The gold must be recovered — more, we must find out who took it, and how.'

He paused, clearing his throat.

'I'd be glad of suggestions for further action,' Crispian said quietly.

The Commissioner thought for a long time, finding it impossible to suggest anything new. The bullion might have vanished into the air of its own accord, so improbable was it that anyone could rob the Bank of England.

'It must have been an inside job,' he said abruptly.

Crispian shook his head.

'I've checked on every single person connected with the strongrooms. It would have needed a conspiracy between staff and guards and either the Governor himself or Beadnell. And even then the secret could not have been kept. I'm positive we can rule out the staff.'

'But no one else could get into the vault,' the Commissioner said irritably.

'Quite so, sir — in the ordinary way. But this is no ordinary case. I'm thinking of the reports we've had lately, of men who walk through walls. The Ghosts, as the newspapers call them.'

The Commissioner snorted.

'Are you suggesting that someone

walked through solid stone walls, and out again, with a million pounds in gold bullion? It's fantastic!'

'No more fantastic than what has actually happened,' Crispian returned. 'I don't think we'll ever explain it by ordinary means.'

'So we're up against the supernatural! Is that what you believe, Inspector?'

'No, sir, not the supernatural. Remember, one of our ghosts took a meal from a restaurant in Soho, and that argues a material body. I think we're up against a scientific criminal, one who has some new invention for penetrating solid obstacles. With your permission, sir, I'd like to call in a scientist to report on the possibility.'

'It's far-fetched, no doubt, but — ' The Commissioner considered the idea. He was a heavily built man with a habit of frowning when he was worried, and just now the furrow between his brows was deep indeed.

'If you're right,' he said, breaking a long silence, 'this sort of thing could go on. Damn it, Crispian, we've got to crack this case, and fast. Who do you want?'

'Professor Eurich.'

'Eurich, eh?' The Commissioner toyed with a paperweight. 'I remember him — he helped you solve the Robertson affair. A good man, I believe.'

'That's right, sir. A first-rate scientist, and well up in police procedure.'

The Commissioner turned the conversation again.

'The leaf you found in the Bank's vault — you say it came from South America? That's a long way. Do you think it was placed there to mislead us?'

'I don't think so,' Crispian answered slowly. 'I've a hunch our man left it without knowing he did . . . and that only makes the problem tougher.'

'All right,' the Commissioner decided. 'You'll get your scientist — now get busy.'

3

Murder

Crispian found little time to devote to the scientific aspect of the case for other sensational robberies followed in quick succession.

The first occurred on the premises of a jeweller in Hatton Garden. Diamonds, rubies and emeralds were taken from a safe behind a steel grille in a locked room. The night watchman heard nothing and the theft was not discovered till morning.

Crispian and his men searched the room thoroughly, without finding any clue to explain how the jewels had been removed. Private detectives hired by the insurance company had no more success. Then came the report of a similar robbery in Paris and Crispian flew over to France to investigate.

★ ★ ★

A telephone shrilled in the early hours of the morning. The Curator of Antiques at the British Museum stirred in his sleep and groped for the receiver.

'The entire contents of a cabinet of Inca relics have disappeared,' said the urgent voice of a keeper. 'They were still there two hours ago when I passed through the room. I can't understand how the thieves broke in . . . '

The curator dressed quickly and hurried through the deserted squares of Bloomsbury; his echoing footsteps were the only sounds in the silence and starlight cast a silver sheen over roofs and trees. He let himself into the Museum and passed through one room after another till he came to the gallery where the Inca relics had been displayed.

The keeper was waiting for him. 'I don't understand it,' he said, shaking his head. 'The case doesn't appear to have been tampered with, yet the things have gone.'

One glance was enough for the curator. The cabinet, which had contained finely wrought figures in gold studded with precious gems — priceless works of art by master craftsmen, impossible to replace — was now empty. It was still locked and the glass intact.

'This is a job for Scotland Yard,' the curator decided, and went to his office to telephone.

★ ★ ★

They unsealed the massive doors and Detective-Sergeant Williams walked into an empty vault under the Royal Mint and stared gloomily about him. He saw bare walls and bare shelves where, a few hours before, valuable bars of silver had been stored.

I should be getting used to this, he thought. Of course, it's impossible — and there won't be any clues!

He made a methodical search, testing everything for prints. The warning system had not operated and the doors showed no signs of having been forced. There was no other entry to the vault.

He inspected the metal grilles over the air ventilating ducts, but they had not been touched. Irritably, he stared round the vault; the walls were solid and armed guards patrolled in the corridor outside. It was impossible for anyone to have got in . . .

Sergeant Williams thrust his hands deep into his pockets and swore.

'Not even a ruddy leaf this time!'

How the blazes could anyone get silver bullion out of the Mint? Unless he were invisible and walked through walls Williams was fast reaching a state of mind where he was prepared to believe in — The Ghosts.

He settled down to question the staff; and learnt precisely nothing.

★ ★ ★

Inspector Crispian arrived back from France with a feeling of frustration. He strode into his office at New Scotland Yard to find Williams reading the latest edition of the *New York Times*. Crispian scanned the headlines as he dropped into his chair.

INTERNATIONAL CROOKS STRIKE AGAIN
DARING ROBBERY ON WALL STREET

'Any luck?' Williams asked hopefully.

'Nothing. And you?'

The sergeant shook his head.

'The trouble is,' Crispian said, 'we're chasing our own tails! We've nothing to work with, no leads to follow. What we need is a completely new approach to the whole business. It's hopeless even to expect to trace the stuff; famous art treasures can't be disposed of on the open market, neither can bullion in large quantities — and no ordinary fence would touch the jewels that have been stolen.'

'What baffles me,' Williams commented, 'are these reports of a man dressed in a white tunic, with a beard and deformed face. Surely one man alone can't be responsible? It would take a well-organized gang to operate in London, Paris and New York in quick succession. So why this fantastic disguise?'

'I don't know.' Inspector Crispian looked down at the bulky file on his desk and sighed. 'I don't know, Bill — but one thing is certain, we've got to have scientific help if we are to stop these crimes. I'm going to see Professor Eurich right away.'

★ ★ ★

Mary Marshall kicked off her shoes, threw herself into a comfortable chair and closed her eyes. It was good to put her feet up, to rest a moment, to relax. The small, whispering sounds of the sea floated up from below, merging with the gaiety of the crowds on the beach. She felt utterly exhausted.

It had been her day, her triumph, yet somehow she did not feel part of the celebrations. She needed these few minutes alone to compose herself before dressing for dinner.

She opened her eyes to look down through half-closed Venetian blinds, to the yellow sands and the sapphire-blue Pacific, the dazzle of white crests in sunlight. She was going to miss these things when she returned to England; yet she would be glad to be home again. Los Angeles was wonderful, but life as Miss World was altogether too hectic for a girl used to the quiet of an English village.

She hardly seemed to have had a moment to herself, what with parties lasting through the night, the hours spent posing in her swimsuit, a hurried film test and TV appearance, the photographs and signing of agreements for advertising. She had enjoyed it all, but now she was glad to be going home with her prize money.

A knock at the door brought her back to reality.

'Miss Marshall? The car's waiting downstairs.'

'All right, Harry — I'll be down in ten minutes.'

She couldn't be bothered to hurry . . . she'd relax for a few more minutes.

Harry was a press agent, a courteous young man who had assumed the role of escort during her stay in Los Angeles — a service for which she was grateful as it saved her from the unwelcome attentions of 'wolves'. One or two of these had become so persistent that she kept the door of her suite locked . . .

She closed her eyes again, dreaming of home. Dad would be proud of her success — he had encouraged her to make the trip to California, in spite of village gossip that had threatened to destroy her reputation.

A sombre voice said: 'The judges deserve to be congratulated on their choice, Miss Marshall. Truly, you are a most beautiful girl!'

Mary gave a tiny gasp of astonishment and sprang from her seat. She saw the strange figure of a man clad in white; the lower half of his face was masked by a thick beard and his eyes glittered as their gaze fixed on her. She stared in horror at the mutilation of the face above the beard — then her natural compassion came to the fore and her feeling turned to one of pity.

'Who are you?' she whispered. 'How did you get here? And what do you want?'

He advanced towards her, and his

laughter had both bitterness and mockery in it.

'Surely you've read about me in the papers, Miss Marshall? Locked doors mean nothing to me. As for what I want, the answer is . . . *you*!'

He seized hold of her and, though she struggled, she could not break free. He was incredibly strong and lifted her off her feet as if she were a child.

'Put me down,' she cried out.

He carried her across the room, moving towards a blank wall. Mary kicked and screamed, for she felt sure that she was in the hands of a maniac. He adjusted some mechanism at his waist and the room faded to a grey haze; walls and floor shimmered as though no longer solid.

Mary Marshall became frightened. Her abductor did not stop when he reached the wall. He marched straight into it, through it, as though bricks and mortar had no existence. The shock was too much for her and she fainted.

★ ★ ★

Professor Eurich was short of stature, a fragile, mincing man with a wide forehead and receding hair. He flourished a pair of pince-nez spectacles as he spoke and his manner was that of a lecturer in the classroom.

'Yes, yes, Inspector, I've read your reports — most interesting, but not, I'm afraid, at all illuminating. Present day science cannot explain how a man may pass through solid matter. The illusion could be created, but no more than that.'

'The disappearance of gold from the Bank of England is no illusion,' Crispian said drily.

'Quite, quite. If you wish to postulate a method for walking through walls, Inspector, then you must also postulate an entirely new physical science. Nothing that I know of can account for such a feat.'

'All right,' Crispian snapped, 'postulate an entirely new physical science! What does that give us? And how do we fight this scientific criminal? These robberies have happened and it is my job to find out how. I must learn the modus operandi.'

Eurich smiled faintly.

'I need time to consider the problem, Inspector — and I can't work without data. Can you arrange for me to be present at your next investigation? There are one or two tests I should like to make.'

Crispian nodded and shook hands.

'I'll arrange it,' he promised.

Williams was angry. He threw down his copy of the *Daily Record* on Crispian's desk.

'A nasty business,' he growled. 'To happen to a nice-looking girl like that . . .'

Crispian knew he was referring to the disappearance of Mary Marshall, and frowned. It was an entirely unexpected development. He placed his fingertips together and looked at his sergeant.

'There's a pattern underlying this crazy business, Bill.' He paused, counting on his fingers. 'First, there was the random interruptions of privacy — my guess is that our super-criminal was experimenting with his invention. Trying it out to see if it worked.

'Second, we have a chain of robberies — each one in circumstances that would make theft normally impossible. He's proved his machine, or whatever it is he uses, and now he's cashing in on it. And note that he doesn't take banknotes, which would be much easier to negotiate. That must mean something.

'Third, an abduction — and he selects the winner of a world beauty contest!'

'No doubt what he has in mind there,' Williams said gloomily.

Crispian began again.

'There's another pattern, too. The leaf we found on the floor of the Bank vault came from South America. The Inca relics taken from the British Museum also originated there, many centuries ago. And Inca treasures are made of gold, and silver, and precious stones — the very things that have been stolen. There must be a connection. The coincidence is too strong for me ... I've a feeling our manhunt will take us to South America before long.'

'I don't fancy that at all,' Williams said. 'A hot country, hot as hell, and swarming with flies and poisonous snakes. Do you think that's where Miss Marshall is?'

Crispian considered the point.

'Could be,' he said slowly.

'Then heaven help her!'

Sergeant Williams began to pace the tiny office. Never before had he felt so completely at a loss. He scowled.

'Eurich wasn't very helpful, was he?'

'Give him a chance,' Crispian protested. 'The man can't work without data.'

'And in the meanwhile, we just sit around and wait.'

But they did not have long to wait. The telephone rang, and a voice said:

'I'm calling from the Stonehaven atomic plant. Our Director has just been murdered — in broad daylight, by a man who vanished before our eyes!'

4

Stonehaven

Stonehaven was extensive. The high wire fence marking the limits of the atomic power station ran for miles along the tarmac road, with the main buildings a huddle of concrete blocks on the horizon. Only the two enormous chimneys of the atomic piles made any impression on that bleak moorland scene — and they towered high into the cloudbanks, catching the light of the afternoon sun.

Crispian drove at high speed, with Eurich beside him and the professor's equipment in the back of the car. Williams had been left behind to investigate another robbery.

'You know anything about the set-up here?' Crispian asked.

'A little,' Eurich replied modestly. 'I had a hand in designing the layout . . . but there's something nagging at the back of my mind, something I should remember about Stonehaven, and can't.'

Crispian arrived at the main gate and stopped long enough to identify himself and his passenger. Special passes issued in London insured that there was no delay. He followed the sign-posted route to the Administration block, passing between laboratories and workshops.

They were shown into an office, where Deputy-Director Ashby was waiting to receive them. Ashby was a lean, spectacled figure in heavy tweeds.

'Glad to see you, Inspector,' he said, shaking hands and looking questioningly at Eurich. 'You've made fast time getting here.'

Crispian introduced the scientist and, instantly, Ashby's attitude changed; it was obvious that he was not pleased to have an outsider brought into his establishment.

'I'm afraid this will prove a wasted journey for the professor,' he said stiffly. 'We have plenty of specialists here — competent men.'

Eurich said nothing.

'Professor Eurich has worked with me before,' Crispin returned lightly. 'He knows police methods, and that gives him an advantage over your atomic experts.'

'Well, the police haven't made anything of it yet,' Ashby said with a forced laugh. 'Not that they've had much chance. M.I.5 stepped in straight away.'

'That's not surprising in a place like this.'

'No, Inspector, you're wrong — it's not like that here. We have a certain amount of security, naturally, but this isn't a secret research station. Stonehaven is concerned mainly with manufacturing atomic by-products — radio-isotopes for industry and hospitals — and so we have no more security than any other organization handling expensive government equipment.'

Crispian was puzzled.

'Then what's upset the Intelligence people?' he asked.

'The manner of the Director's death. It upset me, too — I was one of those who saw it happen.'

As he spoke, Ashby led the way across

the wide expanse of concrete in front of the Administration block, towards the atomic piles. In the shadow of the giant chimneys, between the piles and the chemical laboratories, an area of ground had been roped off. Uniformed police-men patrolled the area, keeping back the curious.

'It all happened so quickly,' Ashby murmured. 'No one could do anything.'

Beyond the ropes, plainclothes men stood in a group round a huddled form lying on the ground. The body of the Director had not yet been removed to the mortuary, though it was now covered by a blanket.

Eurich began unloading his apparatus from the car, while Crispian introduced himself to the local police Superinten-dent. The Super was indignant at having the investigation taken out of his hands.

'About time the Yard stepped in,' he said fretfully. 'I'm tired of being pushed around by M.I.5. This is murder — not a witch-hunt!'

'Just red tape, I expect,' Crispian said. 'I'll try to get some co-operation for you.'

'Blasted red tape!' the Super grumbled. 'What in blazes do these Intelligence men think they know about a murder investigation? They should stick to their own job and leave this to the experts!'

Crispian sympathized briefly and ducked under the rope. He thought: This looks like being tricky — Ashby doesn't like my calling in Eurich, and now the local police are at loggerheads with M.I.5!

The Intelligence man who had taken charge of the proceedings came up to him. He was neatly dressed, square-jawed and clean-shaven with alert grey eyes.

'Glad you've arrived, Crispian,' he said briskly. 'I'm Reynolds — I knew you were engaged on the 'Ghosts' case and asked for you to be sent down. I hope we can work together.'

Crispian relaxed; Reynolds was going to be easy to get on with.

'This isn't just another murder,' the Intelligence man told him. 'The Director of Stonehaven was killed by something that might turn out to be the fabulous death-ray beloved of fiction writers. We want to get our hands on it — and the man behind it. A thing like that can't be allowed to leak through to our enemies. That's why I'm here. This is a matter for top security.'

'All right,' Crispian agreed. 'Give me the picture.'

Reynolds walked across to the corpse and took hold of the blanket.

'This isn't pretty,' he warned.

Crispian braced himself as Reynolds drew back the blanket.

He saw the body of a man in the prime of life, with a head that was scarcely recognizable as such — it was a charred and withered stump. He forced himself to stoop lower and inspect the thing closely.

'Incredible! The head looks as though it suffered intense local heat — yet the clothes of the body are hardly singed.'

'Quite.' Reynolds' voice was grim. 'It happened in a fraction of a second and the weapon was focused on the head. He died instantly, of course.'

'Ashby told me he saw it happen . . . '

'A number of people did, and their reports agree. The Director was walking towards No. 1 pile when a man dressed in a short white tunic materialized about ten yards in front of him. Descriptions of the weapon vary, but it seems to have been shaped like a harpoon gun. The murderer did not speak. He simply aimed his weapon and fired.'

Reynolds opened a packet of cigarettes, selected one and lit it.

'Everyone agrees on what happened next. There was no sound, just a sheet of blinding light — Ashby referred to it as a flash of lightning — and the Director collapsed. Several people started to run towards him, and towards the man in white but he vanished as mysteriously as he appeared. He wasn't there any more.'

The Intelligence man drew hard on his cigarette.

'Any ideas on this vanishing trick, Inspector?'

Crispian shook his head. He looked round, remembering Eurich; the professor was talking to a man in a laboratory coat. Ashby had gone back to his office.

He stared down at the body again.

'Why?' he said suddenly. 'What was the motive behind this murder?'

'That,' said Reynolds, 'is something I'd *really* like to know.'

★ ★ ★

They were sitting silently in the canteen, drinking coffee while they waited for Eurich to complete his tests. Crispian found himself thinking about Mary Marshall; it seemed to him that her position was desperate now that murder had been committed. Reynolds had his eyes shut and was trying to imagine the logical step to take after the routine investigation had petered out from lack of data.

Eurich came in, looking depressed.

'Nothing,' he said. 'No traces of any kind. What I had hoped for was some indication of the type of energy used — assuming a method of passing through solid matter, the energy required would be of a high order. But I drew a blank.'

'No one walked through a wall here, Professor,' Reynolds grunted. 'He just disappeared into the air.'

'It's the same problem — it must be.'

Crispian sighed. 'Another dead end,' he said.

'There is something, though,' Eurich paused. 'All the way down today, I had the feeling there was something I ought to remember about Stonehaven. I've got it now. There was a bad accident here some years ago — it was hushed up, of course, and only the bare facts were reported at the time.

'The control mechanism on one of the atomic piles jammed, and power built up faster than it could be handled. Radiation spilled through the protective walls and a physicist named Ralph Savage was severely burnt. His face was deformed as a result . . . and one night he walked out of hospital and was never seen again.'

Crispian threw off his tiredness.

'And we're looking for a scientific criminal with a deformed face! It can't be coincidence.'

'Revenge motive,' Reynolds snapped. 'How long had the present Director been in charge here? Was he here when Savage was burned?'

'I believe so.'

Crispian and Reynolds exchanged glances. Both had the same thought; they were dealing with a madman out for vengeance.

'Ashby can give us details,' Crispian said, rising to his feet. 'Come on!'

★ ★ ★

Deputy-Director Ashby didn't like it; he seemed to take it as a personal affront that Crispian should want to know about something that had been quietly buried and forgotten.

He moved restlessly about his office, like a wild animal in danger of losing its freedom.

'This is preposterous,' he said. 'Savage can't have anything to do with this murder. He disappeared years ago — why, he's probably dead.'

'But you admit he changed after the accident,' Crispian persisted. 'In hospital, he brooded a good deal on his misfortune and would hardly speak to anyone. We can't know all that went on in his head, but it's likely the balance of sanity was

54

disturbed — and a man in that condition might easily convince himself the Director was to blame.'

Reynolds leaned across the desk to stub out his cigarette.

'It's significant, too,' he added, 'remembering his deformity, that it was the Director's *head* he used as a target. A thing like that would appeal enormously to a man half-mad with thoughts of revenge.'

'I suppose it's possible,' Ashby agreed reluctantly. 'But I don't see how it helps. You've still got to find him.'

There was silence in the Deputy-Director's office; beyond the window, the brightness of electric lights displayed two tall white chimneys against the dark night.

'It always helps to know the identity of the man we're after,' Crispian replied. 'We're not working in a complete vacuum any longer. What we need now are details of his past life, his work, his friends, hobbies, family. We want to know everything about him.'

'I can't tell you much, personally,'

Ashby said. 'I'll put you in touch with the people who knew him.'

Crispian and Reynolds worked hard on the case, but when all the facts were in, information about Ralph Savage was still meagre. It appeared that he had a clean record; he was a first-class worker, his parents had been killed in a car accident and he was unmarried. Savage had been a man without intimate friends. He lived for his work and his social life was almost non-existent. He had been a member of several scientific societies and was respected by his colleagues — and, up until the time of his accident looked like a man who was going to get to the top of his profession.

Crispian checked with the hospital where Savage had been treated after the accident. One of the nurses remembered him. She told them she had heard Savage rambling about taking his revenge on society . . .

Later when they were setting the manhunt in motion, Reynolds said:

'Savage is our man all right — and damned if I don't feel sorry for him. He certainly got a raw deal . . . a top-flight scientist, and then — '

'Forget it,' Crispian said briefly. 'Whatever he was is in the past. Now he's dangerous — and our job is to hunt him down.'

5

The trap

All the way back to London, Crispian was troubled in his mind. It was one thing to know the name of the man he wanted — and he had no doubts now that that man was Ralph Savage — but it was quite another matter to arrest him when he could walk through walls and disappear into the air.

In the privacy of his office at New Scotland Yard, he posed the problem to Eurich and Williams.

'What sort of brain are we up against, professor? Did he invent this new weapon and the trick of materializing himself through solid walls? Or has he picked it up somewhere? Maybe he's one of a gang of scientific criminals.'

'It's a gang all right,' Williams said confidently.

Eurich was more cautious.

'I'm not so sure, sergeant. It's possible, of course — but if Savage has stumbled upon a new theory of physics, he may well be able to perform feats which we would hesitate to assign to one man.' He paused, turning to Crispian. 'At the moment, I've nothing to work on. Stonehaven proved that Savage leaves no detectable trail — I've got to set up my apparatus in advance, knowing where he will strike.'

'He's not likely to tell us,' Williams commented.

'If you could guarantee he will appear at a specified place at a specified time,' the professor continued, 'I might be able to help. You see, no matter what kind of energy he is using, it can be measured — and traced back to its source.'

'We'll need to set a trap,' Crispian said thoughtfully. 'But what sort of bait will he rise to?'

He reviewed Savage's past raids in his mind. Gold, silver, precious gems . . . and Inca treasures.

★　★　★

Lord Duncarse was a personal friend of the Commissioner; he was also a collector of *objets d'arts* — and the prize of his collection was a gold statuette of Inca origin.

Crispian arranged for a craftsman to manufacture a replica in secret; and then advertised the fact that the statuette would be on view to the public at the Arts Council gallery in St. James's Square.

He brought Reynolds into his scheme and they planned the trap in cooperation with Professor Eurich. The room in which the Inca statuette was to be shown was quite small; a curtained alcove would hide the watchers and Eurich's mechanism was concealed in the base-piece on which the figure stood.

'He'll come by night, if he comes at all, after the gallery is closed to the public,' Crispian said. 'We'll alternate watches — you and I, Reynolds, one night, Williams and someone from your department the next. I'll have men covering the building from outside and a fast car standing by. Even if we miss him, he'll only get away with a fake . . . and maybe the professor will secure a reading on his home base.'

★ ★ ★

A clock struck three times and the echo of it was a ghostly sound. Crispian stirred in his alcove, shaking his head to drive away the feeling of sleepiness that threatened to engulf him. He drew back the curtain to peer into the room.

A single shaft of moonlight came through an uncurtained window to reveal the golden statuette framed by its glass cabinet. Crispian had had plenty of time to observe the sun-goddess; even in replica, there was a feeling of barbaric power about the sinuous form. Three feet in height, golden and banded with silver studded with precious gems, the statuette was a tribute to the skill of the artist who had fashioned it. The glass eyes held the cold fire of moonlight.

Beside him in the alcove, Reynolds shredded an unlit cigarette between his teeth. It was their third night on watch and so far no attempt had been made to

61

take the statuette.

The room was quiet and cool and the ebony base under the sun-goddess gave no hint of the machinery Eurich had installed. The trap waited. All that was wanting was the quarry.

Reynolds dropped the remains of a cigarette into his pocket and placed a fresh one between his lips. Crispian shifted his weight and sighed. The clock struck once in the silence.

The high Georgian windows were tight fastened, the door locked. There was absolutely no sound . . .

Reynolds' hand tightened on his arm and Crispian tensed. Across the room, a hazy shape moved, ill-defined and wraith-like. It took on solid form as it passed into the moonlight. A man, dressed in white and wearing sandals, bearded, with the face above scarred and deeply-seamed. Ralph Savage.

Crispian held his breath, excited and a little scared. He had not seen Savage enter the room, had heard nothing. He looked for the weapon that had killed the Director at Stonehaven but could not see it.

Savage approached the statuette and stood before it, motionless, deep in contemplation. He seemed in no hurry. The seconds passed. Crispian thought of the professor's instruments, measuring and recording, and forced himself to wait. Reynolds had drawn his revolver.

Savage reached out to take the statuette. His hands passed through the glass — Crispian saw that distinctly and a slow thrill crept along his spine — and touched it.

'Now!'

Crispian and Reynolds sprang together, ripping away the curtain. Savage turned on hearing them, and adjusted a control at his belt. He brought the sun-goddess out of the glass case without breaking it . . . even as he leapt, Crispian wondered at the miracle.

He seized hold — No, his hands gripped nothing, passing through the empty air where he saw Savage to be. There was no physical contact at all.

Reynolds cursed, brought up his revolver and fired point-blank at the white figure; the bullets had no visible effect and lodged in the wall behind. Savage laughed mockingly as he retreated with his prize. He moved into a solid brick wall and vanished from sight.

Crispian blew three short blasts on his police whistle. Reynolds unlocked the door and both men ran into the hall. There was no sign of Ralph Savage and the men posted outside had seen nothing. A careful search of the area revealed that Savage had got clean away.

★   ★   ★

Professor Eurich tapped at his teeth with the end of a pencil. He looked pleased with himself. He also looked both worried and puzzled.

The first rays of the sun were slanting in over the tops of the houses, showing the shining intricacies of the instruments that had been hidden in the base of the sungoddess. Papers were scattered about the room, leaves torn from the professor's notebook as he calculated and interpreted the meaning of his readings.

Crispian and Reynolds sat waiting for him to speak.

'I have one definite result which will be of interest to you,' he began. 'I can pinpoint the source of energy that Savage is using. It originates from a point situated at latitude 5° 40′ south and longitude 73° 25′ west. The atlas shows this to be an unexplored region in South America.'

'That checks,' Crispian said, thinking of the leaf he had found in the Bank of England. 'I've had a hunch all along that we should have a trip to South America.'

'Beyond that, however,' Eurich continued, 'I can offer little more than surmise. Whatever it is that Savage has, it is completely unknown to present day science — in fact, certain aspects of it indicate a process alien to human thought . . . '

'Alien?' Reynolds echoed. 'What does that mean? That it is the product of an insane mind?'

Eurich hesitated before answering. 'More than that,' he said. 'This weapon reveals a different kind of thought-pattern behind it. Not simply a different degree of human thought — a different kind. The type of energy involved is brand new — at a guess, I should say that inter-atomic forces are present.'

'Savage worked on atomic physics.'

'This is quite different — I doubt if even the basic concept is the same. Energy was beamed from the source I have indicated and picked up by a receiver here in a way I cannot envisage.'

'He had some sort of gadget belted to his waist,' Crispian pointed out.

'Probably the receiver,' Eurich agreed, 'though it seems incredible to me that such power can be controlled by a piece of apparatus small enough for a man to carry around. This discovery, when we have all the relevant data, will open up an entirely new field of research in physical science.'

'That's fine,' Reynolds grunted, 'but what bothers me is how he could walk off with the statuette, yet we couldn't touch him. Surely, there must be some physical agency involved?'

'I can't explain it,' the professor said unhappily. 'I can't tell you any more for the moment.'

He began packing his instruments and notebooks. Crispian rose and stretched himself, yawning.

'Never mind the details, professor — you've done well enough. Now we know where to look for Savage . . . '

Reynolds grinned.

'And isn't he going to be surprised when we drop in on his little hideout in South America.'

The Scotland Yard Inspector and the M.I.5 man looked at each other; both were planning ahead.

'Savage is my responsibility,' Crispian said bluntly.

'You're welcome to him — I want his secret weapons before they get into the wrong hands.'

Eurich looked up, mildly surprised.

'They could scarcely be in worse hands,' he remarked. 'Savage is obviously unbalanced — and he controls weapons which may well wreck our civilization . . . I must warn you that your Savage will not be easily taken, with the forces at his command.'

'Oh, we'll get him, all right,' Reynolds

replied carelessly. 'Don't worry about that.'

But neither man would have felt so confident if they had suspected what lay in the future.

6

Lord of the jungle

The awakening, for Mary Marshall, had the confused quality of a nightmare. She remembered being in her hotel room in Los Angeles, and the unexplained entry of the man with the mutilated face. Then — she couldn't quite believe this — it seemed as though he carried her *through* the wall. After that, a blank period.

And now . . . now she lay on a couch, staring up at a high stone ceiling. Beside her, a young, dark-skinned girl squatted on the floor, fanning her with an enormous green leaf. It was hot; so hot that the heavily-scented air oppressed her and the couch felt like the top of an oven.

Mary sat up. The dark girl smiled and continued to wave her enormous leaf.

The room was composed of stone slabs that had the appearance of antiquity. There was an opening through which she could see the still waters of a lake and, beyond, acres of cultivated land rising in terraces. The sunlight was brilliant, a harsh glare that set the water sparkling.

A volcano smoked and mountains rose steeply to a vivid-green cap that was the jungle. The whole scene was fantastic, like a still from a Hollywood epic. Only the heat was real. She had an intense longing for ice cream . . .

Mary stood up, and the girl rose too. She was, perhaps, fourteen or fifteen, with thick lips and a squat nose, dressed in a short white tunic.

'Where am I?' Mary asked. 'Who are you?'

The girl bowed and spoke rapidly in a language that Mary neither recognized nor understood.

She crossed to the opening and stared over the lake; in the distance men toiled in the fields. Beyond them, a column of metal rose at an angle from the ground, gleaming in the sun.

Mary wondered what it could be.

She stood at the top of a flight of stone steps leading down to the water's edge, with massive columns rising on either side of her. The water looked inviting and, on impulse, she ran down the steps. The heat of the sun struck her anew once she left the shade of the building.

She removed her clothes and dived into the lake, swimming a little way out floating in liquid coolness. The water was clear and still, a luxury to be enjoyed. She turned, looking back.

The building at the top of the steps was a temple, there could be no doubt of that. Majestically proportioned, the stone façade carved ornately, it had the form of a cube topped by a dome. It must have been built a long time ago, Mary realized.

Movement on the steps caught her attention. The dark girl had picked up her clothes and was retreating with them. Mary called to her to stop but the girl vanished inside the temple.

She swam quickly to the steps and found there a simple white tunic and a pair of sandals. Mary relaxed; at least she was not going to be left completely naked. The heat of the sun dried her almost instantly and she dressed and went up the steps.

There was no sign of the girl and she wandered from room to room, till she came to a hall filled with strange machinery. She had never before seen anything like those machines; their shape was distinctly odd and somehow unnerving. She regarded them with awe.

The air in the hall held an electric tension; there was an incessant throb of power. It built up till her head began to ache and she wanted to scream.

The girl returned, speaking excitedly and gesturing with her hands. When Mary did not move, she seized hold of her arm and pulled. Mary understood then that the hall of machines was taboo and not to be entered.

She followed the girl to a small anteroom where food was laid out on a table. The sight of it reminded her that she had not eaten for some hours; she sat down to eat, suddenly hungry. The dark girl renewed her fanning.

'This is quite impossible,' Mary said aloud. 'I shall wake up in a moment.'

There were pancakes that might have been made from potatoes, dark brown bread with a pleasantly crisp flavour, wine in a jug and a bowl of exotic fruits. She had almost completed her meal when a man's deep voice broke in on her.

'I hope you are feeling better, Miss Marshall. Do you have everything you need?'

Startled, she jumped up. It was the man with the deformed face again.

They stood looking at each other in silence; she, nervous and uneasy; he, appreciative of her beauty, yet with a searching intensity in his gaze.

'How do you feel now?' he asked suddenly. 'No ill effects from your journey? It is the first time I have used the machine to transport another person and I wasn't sure what would happen. Tell me if you feel at all unwell.'

Mary experienced an upsurge of anger. Words poured from her lips as if of their own accord:

'How did I get here? You had no right to bring me to this place — I don't like it! *Who are you?* I insist that you take me back at once — I won't stay here another minute!'

He sat down, regarding her with evident amusement.

'You make it clear that you are quite well, my dear.'

'Where is this place?' Mary persisted.

'South America — a somewhat remote part of that continent. And you must accept the fact that you are here to stay . . .'

'South America?' It made some sort of crazy sense, she supposed; at least it explained the tropical heat and the volcano and the jungle-capped cliffs. 'I don't understand,' she said weakly.

He laughed and rose to his feet.

'You are very beautiful,' he murmured. 'Do you remember the old fable of Beauty and the Beast? I hope you are going to like me, Mary, because soon I intend to take you for my bride.'

He bowed, and left without another word.

Mary did not intend to cry but, somehow, she could not stem the flow of tears. It's stupid of me, she thought — crying won't help. I've got to persuade him to return me home.

The days passed in endless succession. Each day appeared the same as the last and Mary had little hope that the next would prove any different. She had nothing to do — all the cooking and housework was done by Indians — and time hung heavily on her hands.

She swam in the lake twice a day. In the evenings, she walked alone. During the midday heat, she rested, with the Indian girl fanning her. They were long days, full of boredom and frustration, an interlude — she told herself — after which she would resume her old life. She became bored with her existence and a subtle lethargy stole over her.

Escape was impossible. The Indians left her alone and, anyway, she could not converse with them. There were moments when she was almost glad of the company of Ralph Savage, such was the intensity of the loneliness she knew.

No longer was she startled by his sudden appearances, or the riches with which he returned from his periodical trips. She had lost her fear of him, but the idea that they were being drawn together by their very isolation worried her more and more. And he seemed to be waiting . . .

She had her own room and, so far, he had made no attempt to interfere with her. He was lonely, too, she guessed; he needed someone to share his dreams — and he was a man of strange dreams. Something in his past, something of which he had yet to speak, had warped his mind. He was like a small boy who desperately wanted her approval.

It could not last, she realized. One day he would tire of waiting, and then —

One evening she returned from swimming in the lake to find him in her room. His deep-set eyes glittered and all his muscles were tensed; even his voice betrayed the depth of his emotion.

'Mary,' he said, 'why put off the inevitable? You must know that I love you. I should like our marriage to take place.'

He was moving towards her as he spoke and he did not wait for an answer. His hands, like immensely strong talons, gripped and held her; his mouth pressed fiercely, demandingly, on hers. She did not try to resist, but submitted coldly, rigid as a marble statue. Abruptly, disappointed, he released her.

'Very well,' he said. 'I can wait.'

'Mr. Savage,' Mary said quietly, 'my father will be worrying about me. Will you please let me go?'

'Never,' he told her. 'I shall never let you go.' He paused. 'If you wish to reassure your father, write a letter telling him you are happy here. I'll see it is delivered.'

Mary sighed.

'I'll write,' she said.

★ ★ ★

It was difficult to know what to put in the letter. Savage would obviously read it, so she could not say what she really felt — that she wanted only to get away from him. Yet she must write something to allay her father's fears.

She tore up several false starts, finally deciding on a brief note.

'I am alive and well,' she wrote, 'and you must not worry about me. I think of you constantly, and know that you think of me. I do not know if I shall ever see you again, but you must not worry because I am no longer afraid of anything the future may hold in store for me.'

When she had finished the letter to her father, Savage read it through and nodded. Mary watched him walk with it to the hall of machines, and it seemed to her like the end of something — a complete break with the past. She felt a different person, with a different life opening up before her. It was then that she began to spy on Ralph Savage.

★ ★ ★

A few days later, as she sat on the terrace and watched the sun set behind the mountains, the sound of an aircraft startled her. She looked up eagerly. Was this, perhaps, someone searching for her?

She saw a moving speck appear over the distant line of cliffs and swoop low across the valley. It was a helicopter, travelling slowly, heading towards the temple and descending all the time.

Savage's voice came from just behind her.

'It seems we have a visitor, my dear. A pity my welcome must be somewhat drastic . . . '

She turned her head, and shuddered at the expression on his face. It boded ill for the pilot of the aircraft.

He entered the hall of machines in long, hurried strides. Mary kept her gaze on the plane, hoping and praying for rescue. From inside the temple came the high-pitched whine of a machine; the very air seemed to vibrate as Savage stepped up the power.

Mary clenched her hands, staring into the sky, watching the tiny craft.

Then, without any visible reason or warning, the helicopter's engine cut out. The plane began to slip sideways, falling . . . falling . . . She could see the stationary rotor blades above the plastic hood of the cockpit, and the pilot trying to struggle free as the crash came. She closed her eyes. There was a noisy rending of metal — and a terrible silence.

Mary held her breath and counted up to ten. When she opened her eyes again, Savage was standing beside her, smiling; and, in that moment, she began to hate him.

'You devil!' she exclaimed, and ran at Savage, beating him with her fists. 'You've killed him!'

Savage laughed, and held her off.

'Not yet,' he said, 'not before I've learnt how he found this valley.'

He motioned to an Indian and spoke several words in the Inca tongue. The Indian ran towards the wreck.

Savage said: 'If the pilot has survived, he will be brought to me for questioning.'

Mary saw other Indians, armed with spears and long knives, converge on the crashed helicopter — and hope died in her. She looked at Ralph Savage with an expression of loathing, and then turned away.

For the moment, she forgot that her chance of rescue had gone; the pilot was hurt and would need medical aid. She prepared hot water and tore some of her clothing into strips for bandages; she made the Indian girl who was her servant bring herbs and potions. When all was ready, she went again to the terrace.

Presently, the Indians returned, bringing with them a prisoner. He was a big man, built like a gorilla, with flaming red hair.

7

Latitude 5° 40, longitude 73° 25

Lima, on the western seaboard of South America, was hot and dusty when Crispian and Reynolds landed at the airport. They had travelled by jet strato-cruiser via the Azores and Panama, and thence down the coast, with the blue Pacific on one side and the peaks of the Andes on the other. They arrived in the full heat of the noon sun.

They hired a cab and drove into the city, passing a contrasting panorama of old and new styles in building. Skyscrapers jostled against the mosaic-tiled patios of early Spanish houses; a bullring lay in the shadow of a vast modern hospital; belfries of Mohammedan aspect vied with baroque churches and glass-fronted multiple stores.

In the flower-decked squares, pigeons alighted on innumerable bronze statues and fountains. Streetcars rumbled and American tourists in gaudy shirts contrasted with veiled Creole women, and streamlined Packards with heavily-laden mules.

They saw the magnificent stores on the *Paseo Colon* and the cathedral, its spire seeming to rival the mountains behind. The University was as modern as any in Europe.

'It's quite a town,' Reynolds observed respectfully, as the cab deposited them at the Hotel Grande in the central plaza.

Their rooms were booked in advance and, after a bath and a meal, they made their plans.

'Lima,' Crispian said, 'will be our base of operations, the springboard to the interior.'

The windows were open and screened from the sun, and an electric fan stirred the sultry air. Both men nursed long, cool drinks.

'Our first need is for detailed information of the locality that Savage has picked for his hideout. I propose, therefore, to carry out a preliminary reconnaisance by air. A helicopter, fitted with long-range tanks, should be best for the job. I'll go alone and report back by radio everything I see. You'll be in charge of base and, if anything should happen to me, use your own judgment. I'll see you have plenty of facts to work on.'

Reynolds lit a fresh cigarette and tossed the old butt into an ashtray.

'My job, I reckon,' he said lazily. 'You stay in Lima.'

'No, I can handle a helicopter. And it's my duty to make the arrest.'

'I have to get hold of those weapons before anybody else.'

Crispian said: 'All right, we'll toss for it.'

He flipped a coin into the air.

Reynolds called, 'Heads.'

'Tails — you stay.'

The Intelligence agent frowned. 'I still don't like this solo idea,' he said. 'I favour a show of force.'

'Not till we know what we're up against. Remember, Savage has weapons of which we know practically nothing — it would be senseless to risk lives at this stage. Besides, alone, I might take him by surprise. If I could get Miss Marshall away, we shan't be handicapped when the real trouble starts.'

'Well, carry a gun and don't hesitate to use it,' Reynolds said. 'I'll be at this end of the radio link, ready to act when you give the word.'

'It should be a straightforward trip,' Crispian argued.

'The professor gave us a very precise fix — all I have to do is fly there, take a look round, and come back.'

'Yeah, that's all. Just make sure you come back!'

★   ★   ★

Crispian took the helicopter up to its maximum ceiling and headed north-east. The Andes made a solid barrier in front of him, snow-capped and formidable. He flew between sheer Cliffs, into a chasm torn by the torrential flood of river water on its way to the sea.

He passed the first ridge of mountains, dotted with homesteads on the lower slopes, and continued over the plateau. Glass-smooth lakes spread out before him, dazzling under a tropical sun; in places, the rivers cascaded over tremendous falls, their spray a rainbow of colour.

Beyond the final mountain chain, the jungle started; it reached to the horizon, a tangled mass of giant trees and creeper and lush foliage, like a vivid green carpet. The only breaks in the jungle were patches of swamp; and, listening to the smooth music of the helicopter's engine, Crispian felt a deep satisfaction. A forced landing now would be the end of him.

He called Reynolds on the radio for a routine check; then took another fix on latitude 5° 40', longitude 73° 25'. The carpet of jungle continued endlessly.

The sky was clear, an intense bowl of blue all around him. Hour after hour, Crispian kept on his course and, as evening fell, he approached his destination.

He called Lima again:

'I'll be over the position Eurich gave in a few minutes. No sign of anything out of the ordinary. Just jungle — and more jungle.'

'I hear you,' Reynolds answered. 'Don't take chances. Let me know the second you spot something.'

'There's a river below — it disappears somewhere ahead. A waterfall I expect. Coming up to latitude 5° 40′, longitude 73° 25′ . . . now!

'The jungle stops at the edge of a precipitous cliff. I am looking down into a small valley ringed completely by high cliffs. There's a lake and a volcano . . . and . . . can't quite make this out. Looks like a metal column, shining bright in the sun. Not natural, I'd say.'

'Watch yourself,' Reynolds said.

'There are Indians working in the valley — the land is cultivated, rising in terraces. At the far end of the lake, a stone temple. I'm going down . . . '

'Keep talking,' Reynolds said. 'Describe everything. Don't break the contact.'

'The sun is setting behind me. Indians look up as I fly over. No sign of Savage. I'll take a closer look at the temple before I — '

Crispian stopped speaking as the helicopter's engine failed. He juggled

87

with the controls as the machine side slipped, out of control. The ground rushed up at him.

'Reynolds!' he yelled.

There was no answer from the radio; that, too, appeared to have stopped working.

The plane wouldn't handle at all, no matter what he did. Sweat poured off his brow.

'Engine stopped,' he reported, with little hope of being heard. 'I'm crashing . . .'

He struggled to open the hood of the cockpit, staring up at the stationary rotor blades. He wasn't going to get clear in time. The ground was a crazily tilted wall straight ahead.

Metal shrieked and the whole fuselage shuddered at the impact. Crispian was thrown forward, his head striking the instrument panel. He knew a moment's pain — then a black pool opened up to engulf his consciousness.

★ ★ ★

When Crispian opened his eyes, he was lying on the ground and surrounded by Indians. Automatically, his hand groped for his revolver, and found it gone. He turned over and looked at the wrecked helicopter; one glance told him it would never fly again. He had been lucky to get out alive.

The sharp point of a spear prodded him. He scrambled upright, feeling himself all over for broken bones. His head ached and there was dried blood on his face, but he appeared to have sustained no serious injury.

A spear prodded him again and he stumbled forward. The Indians fell in around him and they started towards the temple. Crispian realized he had fallen into the hands of no ordinary tribe of jungle savages; these men were tall and well-built and dressed in clean white tunics. They carried themselves with a haughty air and their weapons were metal and fashioned by craftsmen.

They moved round the lake and he caught another glimpse of that tantalizing metal column. It rose up at an angle and was rounded at the summit — it must be over three hundred feet high, Crispian calculated. He pondered on its purpose.

Approaching the temple, he saw two figures standing on the terrace; they were still far off but he felt sure that one was a white woman. The temple dominated the valley, a solid stone structure topped by a large dome. The façade was carved with fantastic designs and had an appearance of great antiquity.

Crispian climbed the steps leading to the temple and saw, waiting for him in the shadows, a man and a woman.

Though he had never met Mary Marshall, he recognized her instantly from newspaper photographs — but not one of the pictures had done justice to her beauty. Tall and graceful with fair hair and delicate features, she looked like a goddess against the ancient stone of the temple.

The man was undoubtedly Savage, and Crispian gave the professor full marks for discovering his hideout. Lean, almost to the point of gauntness and dark-tanned by the sun, Ralph Savage stood looking at him. He wore a small black box belted at his waist and carried a weapon shaped like a harpoon gun. His beard was thick and hid the line of his jaw; his eyes were deep-set and glittered like sunlight on glass. The top of his face was hideous, the flesh seamed and pitted as if some wasting disease had ravaged it.

No one spoke. Then one of the Indians handed Savage the revolver he had taken from Crispian; Savage flung it into the lake.

'I remember you,' he said. 'You were one of the men who attacked me when I took the fake sun-goddess. Now the position is reversed — except that you cannot escape! Suppose you tell me how you managed to find me?'

Crispian ignored him and turned to the girl.

'I am Detective Inspector Crispian of New Scotland Yard. You are, I imagine, Miss Mary Marshall?' She nodded. 'Are you all right?'

'I'm a prisoner here — otherwise I'm unharmed.' She saw the blood on his face, and added: 'Let me dress your injuries, Inspector.'

'Later.' Crispian swung back to face Savage. 'It is my duty to arrest you,' he said quietly. 'I advise you to surrender. You are known to be in this valley and considerable forces are standing by at Lima — they will attack if I do not return with Miss Marshall. Give yourself up and — '

'You fool!' Savage jeered. 'It is I — not you — who is the master of this situation — your armies cannot touch me!'

'You murdered the Director at Stonehaven . . . '

Mary gasped: 'I didn't know that.'

'You will stand trial,' Crispian continued evenly. 'However, there can be little doubt that the accident you suffered at the atomic plant has disturbed the balance of your mind — you should escape the full penalty with a plea of insanity. Besides, you are in a strong position. M.I.5 doesn't want the weapons you have to fall into the hands of a foreign power. You would do well to surrender now.'

Savage laughed scornfully.

'I am in a stronger position than you know, Inspector,' he retorted. 'I have weapons which can reduce your cities to rubble and your armies to dust . . . but you still haven't told me how you came to find this valley.'

'One of our scientists traced your source of energy when you removed the replica of the sun-goddess from St. James's Square. Every move you make can be tracked — '

'So! You set a trap for me, Inspector — that was clever of you. But it was not so clever of you to fall into it yourself!'

'You can't escape,' Crispian said doggedly. 'Better to give yourself up now.'

'Fool!' Savage's eyes glittered. 'I fear no one. Very soon I shall take the next step in my plan to make myself ruler of the world.'

'You can't fight the full weight of the civilized world — '

'Civilized!' Ralph Savage spat the word as if all the disgust he felt were contained in it. He thrust his mutilated face close to Crispian's. 'You see what your so-called civilized world has done for me . . . well, now, I am in a position to strike back and, when I have finished with your society, it will be at my feet.'

Crispian said: 'That was an accident. You can't reasonably blame — '

Savage cut him short. 'I am no longer a reasonable man, Inspector. And you may be quite sure I shall exact full revenge for my — accident!'

He turned abruptly and strode off, leaving Crispian alone with the girl.

8

The spaceship

Crispian woke refreshed the following morning. His head was clear and he studied his surroundings with new interest as he calculated the chances of outwitting Ralph Savage and bringing him to justice. There were many things he had to learn before he could make a plan of action — and Mary Marshall could help.

He had to admit the girl surprised him; he was prepared for her good looks, of course, but not for her intelligence and cool handling of the situation. Savage waited for her to respond — and she kept him waiting, playing him like a fish at the end of a line. The efficient way in which she had treated and dressed his injuries revealed to Crispian that here was no ordinary glamour girl with her head full of Hollywood fantasies. His admiration grew steadily.

Savage had assigned two Indians to watch him; both were tall and well-muscled and armed with sharp spears. Crispian didn't feel like antagonizing them. They followed him on to the terrace overlooking the lake as he joined Mary for breakfast.

She looked up and smiled as he appeared.

'Good morning, Inspector,' she said. 'How are you feeling today?'

'Fine,' Crispian replied, dropping into a seat. 'Ready for action. Tell me, do these Indians understand English? Or can we talk freely?'

'They won't understand you,' she said.

Crispian began a breakfast of fruit juice and pancakes. 'There will almost certainly be an attack by air on this valley sometime soon. Reynolds — that's the M.I.5 man working with me on this case — is in Lima and he'll be organizing something now. I want to find out as much about Savage's weapons as I can. I want to start him talking.'

'That shouldn't be difficult,' Mary said. 'He's lonely and needs an audience.'

'Another thing, Mary. I'm going to try to get Savage away from the temple. While we're gone, do you think you could bring up my revolver from the lake?'

'I'll try.'

'Good. If you succeed, dry it thoroughly and keep it hidden. If we get the chance, we may be able to take Savage by surprise.'

The girl looked thoughtfully at him, then asked: 'Do you really think we'll get away from here?'

Crispian laid his hand over hers on the tabletop.

'I'll get you away,' he said quietly. 'Savage may seem to be master of the situation for the moment, but it can't last. You'll see — you'll be home again before many days have passed.'

'That's wonderful . . . I'd almost given up hope, but with you here, well . . . I feel a lot better, Inspector!'

'My Christian name,' Crispian replied, 'is Arthur. I'd hate it if you went on calling me 'Inspector'.'

'Very well, Arthur.'

'About these Indians now. Just how much of a hold does Savage hold over them?'

'They're Incas — '

'Incas!' Crispian was startled. 'I thought they'd died out centuries ago.'

At that moment, Savage came on to the terrace. He was looking pleased with himself. 'So you are interested in my people, Inspector? Let me assure you that they are, indeed, descendants of the original Inca tribe. A remarkable race of craftsmen — I shall be delighted to show you some of their work.' He paused. 'You are well, Mary, my dear?'

'Quite well, Mr. Savage.'

Savage smiled and again addressed himself to Crispian.

'I imagine that the ancestors of my people retreated to this hidden valley to escape extinction at the hands of the Spanish invaders. You will admit they could not have found a better place. Since then, they have had no contact with the rest of the world — my advent here caused quite a stir, and I capitalized on this. Indeed, with my scientific knowledge, it was not difficult to persuade them I was some sort of god come to rule over them. The position has worked out very well.'

'But it can't last,' Crispian said sharply. 'Even with the weapons you possess, you can't expect to defend this valley indefinitely. You will be beaten in the end.'

Savage laughed softly.

'I think not, Inspector. You have still to grasp the full extent of my powers. Come, I will show you round.'

Crispian rose, exchanged a glance with Mary and followed Savage down the steps of the temple. They walked in silence a little way, then Savage said:

'You must not allow yourself to become too attached to Miss Marshall. She is very lovely, and I have no doubt you approve of my choice — but be careful. I should hate to be forced to kill you before that becomes absolutely necessary.'

Crispian started. It had not occurred to him that he might fall in love with Mary, but Savage's words found an echo in his heart. She did rouse feelings in him that no other woman had roused. If he succeeded in saving her from Ralph Savage, anything might be possible. At least, he began to hope so.

He looked back at the temple and saw

the gleam of her white body as she dived into the lake. He hoped Savage had forgotten about the revolver . . .

They approached the Inca village. The houses were well-built and neatly laid out in regular streets, leading off from a central square. Here, great piles of gold and silver bars and jewels lay scattered as if of little value.

'Raw material for my artists to fashion into works of beauty,' Savage said, waving his hands to indicate the loot of a dozen cities. 'Till now, they have been handicapped by a shortage of gold and precious stones — I have changed that. In time, the Incas will achieve again the greatness of their ancestors.'

Crispian studied the Indians carefully; certainly they were not untutored savages. Their dress, their agriculture, their noble bearing all pointed to an ancient civilization. And the Incas of old had been great artists.

Savage pointed to a group of craftsmen at work.

'Do you recognize that piece, Inspector?'

Crispian saw the replica of Lord Duncarse's sun-goddess — a sinuous, feminine figure resplendent with gold paint and coloured glass.

'They are using it as a model for a statue ten times the size of the original,' Savage commented. 'My own idea. Perhaps, when it is finished, I will allow them to sacrifice you . . . the opening ceremony, as it were. I'm sure you'll appreciate the irony of the situation — and it will solve the problem of what to do with you when you cease to amuse me!'

They continued past the village, heading towards the shining metal column Crispian had seen earlier.

'What is it?' he asked.

'You may well ask, Inspector . . . it is a spaceship!'

Crispian stopped dead in his tracks, staring at Savage, and wondering if he heard aright.

'A spaceship?' he echoed.

'You are surprised? Did you think, then, that I invented the weapons I have used against society? No, Inspector, I am not so clever as all that — in fact, I doubt if any human brain could have conceived them. They are alien.'

Crispian was stunned by this knowledge, even though it bore out the opinion of Professor Eurich.

'This ship has crossed space from another world,' Savage continued. 'I am busy learning the secrets of our interplanetary visitors and, when I solve the final mystery, the world will be mine for the taking. So, you see, your threat of attack does not alarm me. Quite the contrary — I welcome the opportunity of testing my strength!'

As he approached the spaceship, Crispian saw that it was even larger than he had first suspected, an enormous cylindrical structure towering high above him. It leant at an angle and had the air of a derelict. The walls were smooth and silvery, tapering to a rounded summit. At ground level, a circular opening gave entrance to the interior.

A vessel from another world, Crispian thought — and the wonder of it gripped him.

'Undoubtedly something went wrong at the time of landing,' Savage said. 'There can be no other reason for the ship being here — though how long ago it came, or what happened to the crew I have no idea.'

He climbed inside, and Crispian followed him.

They stood at the bottom of an immense shaft, the only light entering by the port behind them; high above, the blackness was absolute. The shell seemed to be completely empty.

'When I first discovered the spaceship,' Savage said, his voice echoing hollowly, 'it was filled by machines — strange machines whose purpose I could not even guess. These I had removed to the temple for my convenience, to study at my leisure.

'There was no ladderway, no provision of any kind to enable the crew to move from one level to another. From which I deduce that our visitors were not human in form . . . '

Crispian had the feeling he was in the presence of something beyond all human experience. A coldness descended on him and perspiration made his hands clammy. He had a sudden desire to run, to get away from this alien thing.

'When we return to the temple,' Ralph Savage said, 'I will show you some of the machines and explain their operation. You already know that I have partly succeeded in fathoming their secrets.'

They went outside, and Crispian stood a moment, looking back at the spaceship; he wondered who had piloted it — and where it had come from. And what sort of creatures they were who had crossed the gulf between planets.

He stared up at the intense blue sky, and — in his imagination — beyond, to the cold, dark depths of space. Somewhere out there, among the myriad stars, another race had solved the problem of interstellar flight. It was a sobering thought.

9

The attack

The temple looked cool and inviting as Crispian mounted the steps. His face was turning red from exposure to the sun and beads of sweat glistened in the stubble on his jaw. The air was heavy with a sickly scent and the distant line of cliffs wavered behind the shimmering heat. He was glad to be in the shade once more.

Mary sat in the shadow of a stone pillar, fanned by her dark-skinned Inca girl. As he passed, Crispian glanced quickly at her — and was rewarded with the briefest of nods. He followed Savage into the temple with renewed hope.

The hall where Savage had installed the machines from the spaceship was circular and rose to a lofty dome. The machines were a bizarre lot, each different yet with the same underlying rhythm of metal whorls, like so many gigantic seashells.

Crispian was disturbed by their appearance, so obvious was it that they had not been fashioned by human hands.

The very air pulsed with a sense of power. There were no cables or control switches, none of the familiar instrument dials or coloured displays that make one of Earth's power stations look like any other. Crispian was face to face with the end products of a completely alien technology.

He stared at the machines without comprehension; their purpose was as mysterious as their construction.

'Out of your depth, Inspector?' Ralph Savage asked. 'I'd be surprised if you weren't. It took me almost a year of continuous study to grasp the basic principle involved — and I am a trained scientist. Each machine takes its energy direct from the air around it, the fundamental energy of the universe, the inter-atomic forces which bind all matter.'

He paused, scowling, and his deformed face became even more hideous.

'Don't think there is any connection here with the crude release of power in our atomic plants — there is no breakdown of nuclei, no lethal radiation. A much more subtle process is involved. You are no doubt aware of the physical theory of matter; each atom mainly consists of electrons revolving about a central core made up of protons and neutrons, and the whole system is balanced by invisible forces. It is these inter-atomic forces which are utilized by our interstellar visitors.

* * *

The lake was mirror-calm and reflected the deep blue of the sky. On the terrace, Crispian and Mary talked in low tones.

'Arthur,' she said, 'Your revolver is in my room when you want it — under my pillow. I took out the bullets and wiped them, and pulled cotton waste through the barrel. I think it will still fire.'

Crispian looked sideways at the two Inca guards standing in the shadows.

'I'll have to wait my chance, Mary. Can't do anything till I shake off my watchdogs.'

'Do you have a plan?' she asked.

'No. It's a question of taking any chance that comes.'

He cocked his head to one side, listening intently. He thought he heard —

'Aircraft!' Mary exclaimed suddenly.

They watched the sky and, in the southwest, three black specks appeared, travelling fast. As the sound of their jets increased, Savage came on to the terrace. He spoke tersely in the Inca language and the two Indians seized Crispian and held him fast. Savage disappeared into the hall of machines.

The black specks rapidly became three monoplanes, screaming low over the valley. They turned, wing-tip to wing-tip.

Abruptly there was no sound in the sky. The noise of the jets cut off as though at the turn of a switch. Then there were no planes at all . . . only minute fragments of debris floating down to earth . . . and the bodies of the crews falling . . . falling . . .

There was a long silence. Mary gave a little sob and closed her eyes. A shudder racked her body. Crispian swore bitterly; not one of the airmen could have survived. He hoped Reynolds had not been among them.

A few seconds elapsed before Savage returned to the terrace.

'You see, Inspector. They can't touch me!'

Mary would have thrown herself upon him had not one of the Incas prevented her.

'You devil!' she said hoarsely. 'You murdered them . . . ' Ralph Savage did not seem to hear her words. He stood gazing across the valley, savouring his triumph.

'Nothing left,' he murmured, 'nothing at all.'

Crispian licked his lips. He felt sick — and scared.

'What happened?' he asked. 'How did you do it?'

'Resonance, Inspector — a simple thing like resonance! I broadcast a powerful vibratory beam of a frequency calculated to induce sympathetic vibration in every molecule of the aircrafts' structure.' Savage paused. 'I expect you are familiar with the parlour trick of shattering a wine glass with the note of a violin. Precisely the same principle is involved here. Literally, the planes shook themselves to pieces. Effective, isn't it?'

Effective — and ruthless, Crispian thought grimly. He began to wish the alien spaceship had never landed on Earth.

'That's only one of the weapons in my armoury,' Savage added. 'I have others, even more deadly, as the peoples of Earth will find out before long. My revenge is certain — as certain as that night follows day!'

Crispian shuddered. There was no defence against weapons like these, no defence at all. Savage was smiling.

'I hope this brief reversal won't stop them trying again,' he murmured. 'I really do need to test my weapons before I make the final attack.'

He's mad, Crispian thought dully, *mad* . . .

★   ★   ★

It was late, and a soft breeze carried the scents of a tropical night. The moon, a silver orb, hung in a sky of velvet studded with sparkling stars. It was a night for romance.

Crispian walked with Mary by the edge of the lake, watching the breeze stir and ripple the surface of the water. The mountains had an impressive grandeur by moonlight and the alien spaceship made a single shaft of silver pointing to the stars.

Crispian was acutely aware of being beside Mary, conscious of the perfection of her body, the excitement of her perfume and sheen of her hair. He had never before been so alive to another person's presence, and it gave him incredible happiness just to be near her.

Savage was right, he thought; I am falling in love . . .

He was silent for long minutes, depressed by the idea that he could never mean as much to her as she meant to him. He imagined she must think him ugly, while she — she grew more lovely in his eyes with each passing second.

Suddenly, Mary slipped her hand into his and smiled.

'What is it, Arthur?' she murmured.

He gripped her hand tightly, feeling an intense compulsion to tell her. His words spilled out in a rush.

'I'm a direct sort of person, Mary. I can't make fine phrases — I have to say it outright. I . . . I've fallen in love with you.'

It sounded silly when put into words, none of which had any real connection with what he felt inside him. There weren't any words for that. He expected her to laugh, but her face was perfectly serious when she spoke.

'I know,' she said simply.

Crispian stopped dead in his tracks, still holding her hand and turning her to face him.

'You know?' he repeated incredulously. Then, after a pause: 'I don't suppose you could ever care for me?'

'Are you so sure of that?'

She tilted back her head, lips parted, waiting for him. The moon was large behind her golden head and the night still as if the whole world had been created for this moment. Crispian took her in his arms and kissed her hungrily.

'My darling,' he whispered. 'My darling, how I love you! Mary — '

She clung to him, returning his passion, and time stood still. Behind them, an Indian glided past, silent as a shadow. Mary pushed Crispian from her, pale and frightened.

'Not now, Arthur,' she said. 'Not here. If Savage were to find us, he'd kill us!'

'Damn Savage!' Crispian retorted explosively. 'Damn him to hell!'

'I know, darling, that's just how I feel, but we must wait. Wait till this is all over and we're away from him. Then — '

'Yes?' Crispian said eagerly. 'Then — ?'

Her manner changed instantly. She laughed and began to pat her hair into place. She was suddenly mature, serenely composed, as if something she had long expected had at last happened.

'Perhaps, Arthur,' she said absently. Perhaps . . . '

10

Escape

Crispian started out of a deep sleep as a hand shook him. Moonlight flooded the room and he saw Mary Marshall standing over him, the revolver in her hand.

'Our chance has come,' she said calmly. 'One of your guards is asleep — the other is with my maid.'

Crispian sat up and dressed quickly. He inspected his revolver; it appeared to be in good condition. He loaded it and stood up.

'Savage has his bed in the hall of machines,' Mary said. 'You must shoot him while he sleeps — there is no other way.'

Crispian stared at her, shaken. Her tone of voice was without feeling, as if she did not realize the enormity of the thing she suggested.

'I can't kill anyone in cold blood,' he

replied quietly, 'not even Savage. I must give him the chance to surrender.'

Mary shook her head vigorously.

'You must!' she said. 'He didn't give the crews of those three planes any chance. He's mad . . . evil! You wouldn't hesitate to shoot a mad dog, would you? Savage is like that. There's no telling what he plans to do with his infernal weapons. He thinks only of one thing — revenge! I'm not sure he wouldn't destroy the whole world if he could.'

She stepped closer and gazed into his eyes with an intensity that unnerved him.

'Arthur,' she said quietly, 'I'm serious about this. I've been here longer than you and I know more about him. He isn't sane . . . I've a feeling that if we don't kill him now, while we have the chance, then terrible things will happen.'

Crispian felt uncomfortable.

'I can't do it, Mary.'

She gripped his wrist and led him from the room. Outside, an Indian lay snoring on the floor. There was no one else about. When they reached the entrance to the hall of machines, she stood aside, looking at him. Crispian took a deep breath and stepped inside.

There were shadows everywhere, and bright moonbeams, and the insistent hum of machinery. He saw Savage's bed and moved towards it, his gun levelled. He stooped to waken the sleeper — but the bed was empty.

He turned, staring into the shadows, suspecting a trap. Where was Savage?

Mary's urgent whisper came to his ear: 'What's the matter?'

'He isn't here.'

She was silent; then, with the same demoralizing calmness, said:

'He must be on one of his raiding trips. Do you think we can destroy these machines before he returns?'

Crispian looked doubtfully at the strange forms of the alien machinery.

'I don't see how,' he began. 'It's not as if — '

'Never mind,' Mary interrupted. 'There's no point in waiting for him — we couldn't touch him in his immaterial state. We must escape and pass on our information.'

'That won't be easy,' Crispian said.

'We're buried in the heart of the jungle, and my helicopter is useless.'

'Savage transports himself by one of these machines. We must do the same.'

Crispian was startled. 'How?'

'I've been spying on him,' Mary returned calmly. 'I think I can work the thing.'

She moved towards one of the machines and studied it intently. Crispian watched her, marvelling — this was the girl Savage had considered purely ornamental, too far below his mental stature to have anything explained to her. Once more he was forced to revise his opinion of her.

The machine was not large. It stood some six feet from the ground and was constructed of a dull, silvery metal. It had the same sea-shell-like whorls of all the other machines taken from the spaceship, and it hummed continuously.

Mary nodded to herself as she scrutinized the labyrinth of interlacing whorls.

'Yes, I recognize the settings. Arthur, are you willing to trust me? I don't know much about it, only what I've seen Savage do. We'll have to take a chance on my remembering correctly, and not coming out inside a hill or something. If anything does go wrong ... well, it's best not to think about that.'

'I'll trust you,' he said. 'Do whatever's necessary.'

The girl's fingers probed the metal, seeming to sink into it. The segments moved, intermeshing. The humming changed to a whine of power that built up in intensity.

Suddenly, a guttural exclamation sounded behind them. Crispian wheeled about and saw a dozen armed Incas come running into the hall. He brought up his revolver and squeezed the trigger — but there was only a metallic click. Cursing, he ejected the dud shell and fired again.

Red flame stabbed out and the noise of the shot echoed loudly through the temple. The bullet sped over the heads of the Incas and ricochetted off the far wall; they came to an abrupt stop.

Crispian waited, gripping his revolver. The Indians stood in a group, muttering among themselves, watching him. It was a tense moment, only needing one bolder than the rest to lead a charge . . .

Crispian sweated, not daring to look at Mary. An Indian shifted — and he swung his gun to cover the man. There was a long moment of hesitation, of suspense, then —

'I'm ready now,' Mary said. She held out her hand. 'Stay close to me, Arthur.'

He took her hand and, together, they stepped up to the machine. The air throbbed with power. There followed a feeling of weightlessness, of being suspended in a void — then the room receded in a grey haze and the walls and machines shimmered translucently. The Incas no longer seemed real, but ghostlike, fading into the background.

Mary whispered: 'I think it's going to be all right.'

And then the temple vanished.

★ ★ ★

There was sunlight, the smell of early morning in the English countryside, a chequer-board of fields and hedges.

Crispian had a panicky feeling that the ground was far below, but he only fell a couple of feet. The turf was springy and he landed unhurt. He helped Mary to her feet and looked about him.

A gentle slope led down to a winding lane and, beyond the trees, he glimpsed the top of a church steeple. The scene was incredibly peaceful and, for a moment, he had difficulty in believing that, seconds before, he had been in an Inca temple in the wilds of South America.

He took a deep breath, revelling in his new freedom.

'You're a wonder, Mary,' he said with heartfelt relief. 'I doubt if Savage could have managed it better. Do you have any idea where we are?'

She tossed back her head, blonde hair rippling in the wind, and laughed.

'Of course! This is Suffolk, and the village you can see through the trees is Long Prior, where I was born. Come on, it's only five minute's walk to my home . . . won't Dad be surprised!'

'I must get to a phone,' Crispian said seriously.

'We have one — and while you're making your call, I'll be cooking breakfast. Bacon and eggs. It seems ages since I tasted bacon and eggs. Race you, Arthur!'

She darted away and Crispian trotted after her. Mary continued to astound him; not content to escape to Lima, or even London, she must bring them direct to her own home. He wondered if he could ever hope to understand her fully.

She was running as carefree as a child, and he saw her pause to look back as she turned in at the gate of a handsome Georgian house. Crispian was conscious of his own dishevelled appearance — his clothes were torn and rumpled and he had a ragged beard starting on his chin. He would have preferred to clean up before meeting Mary's father.

Then he put the thought out of his head — he had more important matters to worry about. There was still Savage to deal with. He must contact London and pass on his news.

★ ★ ★

Ralph Savage frowned as he materialized in the hall of machines. He had just returned from Lima, where he had been spying on the forces gathered to attack him. It had been amusing to watch the soldiers and see the planes lined up, knowing he had nothing to fear from them.

But now, standing once more in the temple, he realized that someone had tampered with the transmitting machine — and he was further annoyed to find the Inca guards missing from their posts. He went quickly to Crispian's room and found it empty.

Cursing, he rushed to Mary's room . . . empty again. A torrent of abuse now poured from Savage's lips. His eyes glowed with the light of madness and his mutilated face contorted in a hideous scowl.

He shouted for the Incas — who seemed afraid to show themselves — and snatched up the incendiary weapon he had used on the Director at Stonehaven. He began an immediate search.

His anger mounted all the while and,

when he did discover one of the Inca guards, it was as much as he could do to control himself. The man would have run away had not Savage used his weapon and melted the stone at his feet. The Indian dropped to his knees, trembling.

Savage questioned him and struck him brutally when he received so stupid an answer. As if Crispian and the girl could have vanished in the hall of machines . . .

But a second Indian told the same story. And a third. Savage was forced to believe the incredible — that bull-headed dolt of an Inspector had somehow learnt to operate the transmitting machine. It was only too likely that he had killed himself, and Mary.

Ralph Savage felt despair. He had set his mind on having Mary Marshall beside him when he ruled the world . . . and now that interfering policeman had ruined everything. He was alone again, and his loneliness was intensified.

Till that moment all had gone well for him, and this setback filled him with rage. He stalked into the hall of machines and looked blackly about him; his body shook with his fury and thoughts of revenge drove him to action.

Lima — that's where Crispian would have gone if, by some fluke, he hadn't killed himself. Suppose, at this moment, they still lived . . . Mary and Crispian together. It was too much; the idea was intolerable.

Savage paced up and down, a gaunt, bearded figure, working himself into a frenzy; jealousy and frustration fed his desire for vengeance. He strode between the ranks of alien machines, beating the air with his fists.

He cried out, in anguish: 'Mary . . . Mary . . . by God, he shan't have you!'

The thought flashed through his mind: Lima must be destroyed.

He knew just what he was going to do, and he threw himself into the task with all his energy. He prepared the machine he would use. The madness was upon him and there was the single purpose burning in him.

Destroy!

This time, the governments of Earth would feel the full weight of his power!

11

Earthquake

'It's a pity that Lutyens is in charge of the inquiry,' the Commissioner said. 'He's a pompous ass, and it won't be easy to convince him of the truth.'

It hasn't been easy to convince anybody, Crispian thought grimly.

They walked into the conference room and took their places at the table. Mary was already there, with the head of M.I.5 and Professor Eurich — it was the first time Crispian had seen her since his hurried trip to London. Security had thrown a screen round her at once. Representatives of the three services were also present, silently waiting for Lutyens to arrive.

It was a mystery to Crispian how Lutyens had got himself appointed chairman of the inquiry. He was certainly not an important member of the government; in fact, his main occupation seemed to be serving on various minor committees — and this affair was too big for him.

Lutyens arrived at last, bustling into the room in an officious manner. He was a portly man, red-faced and clearly aware of his own importance. He sat down immediately, rapped the table with his gavel, and began speaking in a deep, fruity voice.

'Ladies — ' he smiled gaily at Mary — 'and gentlemen. You all know why we are here, so I will not bore you with a recapitulation of the facts. Our business is urgent and of the gravest import. You have, I take it, all read Inspector Crispian's report and the attached comments of Professor Eurich?'

He paused, looking round the table, then assuming silence to mean assent, continued:

'The report is a little — ah — unusual, and it is our duty to sift the facts, to penetrate to the core of the mystery, and make our recommendations to the government. I should point out that many important financial interests are bringing pressure to bear — demanding immediate action — and that we must not waste time on details. A considerable amount of gold and precious stones have been removed from the country and this is obviously of the greatest concern to us all.'

He looked directly at Crispian.

'Do you, Inspector, still maintain that the weapons used by Ralph Savage originated from a spaceship — an *alien* spaceship — that is to say, a vessel which has crossed the void from another planet? Do you seriously maintain this extraordinary statement?'

'I do,' Crispian replied briefly.

'Well, gentlemen,' Lutyens said, looking about him, 'I cannot accept such a statement. We must bear in mind the fact that the Inspector has recently returned from a tropical country, a land of the most intense heat, and it seems only reasonable to suppose — '

'I have been examined by three specialists,' Crispian interrupted. 'Their verdict was unanimous: I am not suffering from sunstroke.'

'Specialists!' Lutyens waved his hand contemptuously.

'Inspector, do you also maintain that *one* man — Ralph Savage — is responsible for these outrages?'

'Yes.'

'Incredible, quite incredible! How could one man operate in London and New York almost simultaneously?'

'I have already explained,' Crispian replied wearily. 'In the inter-atomic state of existence during which Savage operates, there is no sense of time at all.'

'Ah, yes, the inter-atomic state. That, I must admit, is beyond *me*. Professor Eurich no doubt understands such things, but — '

'Inspector Crispian's report accounts for the main problems attending these thefts,' Eurich put in promptly. 'His explanation of the inter-atomic state, as related to him by Savage, is wholly credible. Moreover, I do not believe it possible for such a revolutionary theory of physics to have been evolved by Savage himself — or, indeed, by any other human being. Savage has been without laboratory or workshop facilities; he could not possibly have built such machines in the jungle.'

'Perhaps, professor, *perhaps*.'

'Everything in the Inspector's report is true,' Mary said suddenly. 'There was a spaceship — we both saw it. And the alien machines did come from it. How else can you account for what has happened?'

'No doubt there is some perfectly reasonable explanation,' Lutyens observed drily.

A frown gathered on the brow of the head of M.I.5.

'Mr. Lutyens,' he protested, 'we are here to decide upon a course of action — not to find fault with Inspector Crispian's report. He and Miss Marshall are the only people with first-hand knowledge of the situation, and I propose that we base our actions upon an assumption of its accuracy — until, at least, we have more detailed information.'

Lutyens became flustered.

'Quite, quite,' he said hurriedly. 'We must attack this hidden valley *at once*. I suggest that if we drop a cobalt bomb on the valley, then Mr. Savage will cease to worry us.'

'Oh, no!' Mary exclaimed. 'You can't do that. There are the Incas to consider — they have no share in Savage's schemes.'

'Personally,' Eurich added, 'I doubt if dropping a cobalt bomb will solve anything. The inter-atomic forces at Savage's command are considerably more powerful than anything we have.'

'Nonsense,' Lutyens declared. '*Nothing* can stand against the cobalt bomb!'

Crispian sighed and exchanged a glance with Mary . . . the man was an utter fool!

'I should like to suggest,' the Commissioner began — but his suggestion was never uttered, for, at that moment, an urgent message was relayed to the conference room. It told of disaster as unexpected as it was terrible.

★ ★ ★

Lima came slowly awake to a new day. On the surface, everything was normal; the bells of the cathedral tolled and factory whistles blew; streetcars carried the city's workers and schoolchildren and early-rising tourists; barges moved slowly down-river to the port of Callao.

The sun shone, the sky was clear and innumerable pigeons rested on bronze statues, preening their feathers. It was a peaceful, everyday scene.

But, under the surface, deep down in the rock on which Lima stood, violence was unleashed . . .

The ground rocked and split asunder. There was a sound like a thousand thunderstorms and a gale of hot air rushed up from the earth, carrying the pigeons high into the sky. Terrifying rifts appeared in the streets and the river rose above its banks and poured a deluge of water into the new openings. Again and again the shocks came.

It was as if the foundations of the city were lifted; the air filled with screaming; cars and trams collided; and the bulls in the *Plaza de Toros* added their bellowing to the uproar. The fashionable *Paseo Colón* became a great chasm into which fell buildings and people and trees and animals. Dust rose in a black cloud.

The central *Plaza de Armas* was a chaos of noise and fury, and where the cathedral had once stood was now a heap of rubble, bloodied and desolate. A street filled with struggling people suddenly dropped thirty feet into the ground. Bridges snapped like rotten wood. The airfield, where troops and planes were concentrated for the attack on Ralph Savage, was wiped out — not one plane got into the air.

Still the holocaust continued. The earth's crust wrinkled into giant folds, swallowing up the city of Lima, section by section. Huge crags shot upward and craters formed; new explosions rocked the land. The heat increased.

Lava came bubbling up from below the surface and clouds of steam hissed noisily, blotting out the view. Volcanic ash spurted into the air to settle on the surrounding countryside like white-hot snow. The lurid glow of a hundred fires spread through the thickening gloom. Huge stones were tossed high on invisible jets.

132

No life existed in Lima after the first few minutes; and after an hour, the city itself was gone. When the dust settled and the ground ceased to heave, there was a bare vista of cooling rock, a plain of solidified lava with tiny spurts of steam still rising from a network of cracks and fissures.

The scene was such as Earth must have appeared long before Man developed from his reptilian ancestors, before even the reptiles came out of the sea. Barren rock, hot and newly-formed, treeless and waterless, without soil, a waste . . .

It was as if the proud city of Lima had never existed at all.

★ ★ ★

Crispian left the conference room with Professor Eurich; the one a red-haired giant, the other neat and dapper and wearing pince-nez spectacles. They were both silent as they walked across the courtyard and out into the busy heart of London.

Across the street, where people queued for buses, a news placard announced:

EARTHQUAKE DISASTER

And, over the noise of traffic, came the cry of the newsboy:

'Special edition! Lima destroyed by earthquake, special! Entire population wiped out, read all about it . . . half a million dead!'

'Bad news travels quickly,' Crispian commented.

'A shocking business, Inspector — shocking.'

'I'm wondering, was it only coincidence that our forces to combat Savage were standing by at Lima?'

Eurich shook his head decisively.

'I don't think so,' he said. 'In fact, I'm convinced it was no ordinary earthquake. Savage is responsible for this.'

Crispian regarded him with alarm.

'But, surely, even he couldn't devastate an entire city? It hardly seems possible, yet — '

'You completely underestimate the

weapon he has. It would require only a simple application of the inter-atomic force at his command. I'm afraid there can be little doubt that Savage is behind the destruction of Lima . . . '

Eurich paused to marshal his thoughts.

'Suppose he converted an ordinary piece of stone to the inter-atomic state, and then transmitted it to a point immediately beneath the city. There would be nothing difficult in such a feat. And then suppose he materialized that piece of stone — that is, returned it from the inter-atomic state to normal matter. Can you imagine that, Inspector?'

Crispian said: 'I can believe it possible. But what then?'

'Don't you see, there would then be *two* pieces of solid matter trying to occupy the same position in space at the same time — a physical impossibility. The destructive power of such a situation is beyond calculating . . . there would be a most terrible explosion.'

'Yes.' Crispian thought about it, and he didn't like the picture. 'I can see that now.'

He looked about him, at the cars and the shoppers in that busy street; he imagined the factory and office workers, the docks and homes stretched endlessly across the great city of London. He pictured Westminster and St. Paul's — and Savage doing the same thing here.

He put the thought from him with a shudder.

'Savage is unbalanced,' he said finally, 'there can be no possible doubt of that. We must reach him, and kill him, before it's too late. Mary was right — there is no other way!'

12

Savage strikes again

During the twenty-four hours immediately following the destruction of Lima, public opinion became sharply divided. There were those who said that Savage was responsible and demanded swift retaliation; and there were those who claimed the disaster to be due to natural causes.

Newspapers and commentators throughout the world took sides in the argument, but so little information had been released that the issue became hopelessly confused. A fund to aid survivors petered out when it was realized there were none. Observers, flying over the area, reported that the devastation was complete.

Scientists met to discuss the new inter-atomic forces, and Professor Eurich gave it as his opinion that at least three years work would be necessary to evolve the fundamental mathematics — this before any practical application could be thought of.

And, while the rest of the world talked, the United States, without consulting any other power, acted . . .

A guided missile with a cobalt bomb as warhead was aimed at the hidden valley Savage had made his stronghold. It was fired from a secret base near Panama and instruments checked its flight. The rocket successfully hit the target — there was never any doubt of that — but what happened to it afterwards was not discovered. It simply failed to detonate.

They never repeated their expensive failure.

Moscow radio began a series of broadcasts inviting Savage to Russia; they offered him sanctuary in return for information concerning his new weapons. As if in response to these appeals, a small town outside Moscow was wiped out by a similar earthquake — and the broadcast stopped.

In London, Inspector Crispian found himself in a difficult position. Still officially in charge of the case, but with little prospect of ever making an arrest, he was forced to attend conference after conference at which politicians and scientists ridiculed his report. In fact, if the Commissioner had not stood solidly behind him, it is probable he would have been retired from the force.

Everyone talked — the government, the newspapers, the general public — but nothing was done. And still gold and silver and precious stones continued to vanish from the world's treasuries.

In an interview with the head of M.I.5, Crispian learnt what he had long suspected; that Reynolds was dead. He had been aboard one of the three planes that Savage had destroyed with his vibratory beam.

Mary, after much questioning, was allowed to return home; and it was to Long Prior that Crispian went when he was given a few days' leave. He found the Georgian house besieged by reporters, and the local constable vainly trying to disperse them.

Recognizing the Inspector, they immediately surrounded him, demanding an interview.

'Give us the story, Inspector — what's really going on in South America? Can we quote you on the Lima disaster? How about persuading Miss Marshall to pose for a photograph?'

'I've nothing to say,' Crispian replied grimly. 'And if Miss Marshall wants to be left alone, I suggest that you respect her desire for privacy.'

'Come off it, Inspector! She's *news* — winner of a world beauty contest and kidnapped by Savage. Give us a break!'

Crispian ignored them. He walked up the gravel path to the front door. It was opened immediately by Mary's father, and closed just as quickly.

'Glad you've come, Arthur,' Mr. Marshall said. 'Mary will be pleased to see you. She's in her room — shut herself up to get away from those damned reporters.'

He was an upright man of about fifty, his hair turning grey; a widower who spent much of his time cultivating his garden.

'I'll see if I can shift them later on,' Crispian promised. 'It's too bad you

140

should be bothered like this.'

Just then, Mary came running downstairs. She wore a simple print dress with her hair tied back.

'Hello, Arthur,' she said breathlessly. 'I wasn't sure if you'd want to see me again . . . '

Crispian took her hands and pressed them warmly.

'Then you ought to have known,' he told her.

Mr. Marshall smiled to himself and discreetly withdrew.

'I'm glad,' Mary said softly. 'Arthur — '

But Crispian would not let her finish. He drew her to him and kissed her.

'You're lovely,' he whispered, 'lovely! Mary, I want to spend the rest of my life making you happy.'

She gazed intently at him.

'You're sure? I shocked you by asking you to kill Savage. I suppose you think me cold-blooded, but I'm not really like that at all. I'm glad you didn't have to do it.'

'You're a strange girl,' Crispian said, and laughed.

He slipped his hand into his pocket and

brought out a small jeweller's box. He opened it to reveal a diamond ring.

'You see, I came prepared!' He took her hand. 'Mary, I love you — I didn't think it possible I could love anyone as much as I love you. I want you to be my wife. Will you . . . ?'

'Oh, yes,' she said demurely. 'I've quite made up my mind about that — I'm going to marry you, whether you like it or not!'

Crispian slipped the ring on her finger and kissed her again. Then she seized him by the hand and pulled him after her, out of the room.

'Dad will be delighted,' she exclaimed excitedly. 'Come on — we'll tell him now!'

Mr. Marshall did not seem surprised at the news.

'Well, now,' he said, smiling. 'I must admit I've been expecting something of the sort, ever since you two turned up here. I've even brought a bottle of my best sherry from the cellar for a small celebration. Perhaps we can give the newspapers a story after all!'

Ashby was feeling pleased with himself. He had just received official notification of his promotion; he was now the Director of Stonehaven and in sole command of Britain's major atomic plant.

He looked up from the report he had been reading — the monthly production of radio-isotopes had reached a new peak — and stared through the window above his desk, across a flat expanse of concrete to the twin chimneys of the atomic piles. It still gave him an uneasy feeling when he let his imagination dwell on the incredible energies contained within the piles. If anything should go wrong . . .

But nothing could, of course. The uranium was safe behind a solid wall of graphite, and beyond that was another wall of metal and dense concrete. The reaction was controlled by cadmium rods and, even if they should fail, there were safety rods to operate automatically under gravity. It was impossible for the piles to explode.

Impossible . . .

The clangour of warning bells jolted him out of his reverie. He grabbed for the house phone.

'Give me pile control, quickly, please!'

There was a brief pause, then —

'Pile control here. Director? Something's gone wrong — radiation is leaking like hell! And the reaction rate is climbing, even with the safety rods full in. I can't understand it.'

Ashby ran from his office. As he reached the frist pile, he heard Geigers rattling and saw men struggling into protective clothing. Wayland, the senior physicist, gripped his arm.

'There's nothing we can do, Ashby,' he said tersely. 'You must order complete evacuation immediately, not only the plant but the countryside as well. Both piles are out of control — they're set to boil over any time now. You must hurry!'

Still Ashby hesitated.

'It can't be as bad as that. The safety devices — '

'Have failed utterly,' Wayland finished. 'I can't explain it, but it's a fact. Hurry, man — there's only minutes to spare!'

Ashby, white and shaking ran for the nearest microphone that connected with the plant's broadcasting system. He took a deep breath and forced himself to speak slowly, so that his words should not be misunderstood.

'Attention, everyone. This is your Director speaking. A state of emergency exists and Stonehaven must be evacuated. No one, repeat, no one is to remain behind. The evacuation will be according to Plan B. Repeat, Plan B is in operation *now*.'

Then he operated the siren that would warn the whole countryside of its danger.

From offices and workshops, men and women ran for their lives. Cars and lorries, overloaded and with people clinging to the sides, tore away from the danger zone at full speed. There was tension in the air, a feeling of panic. The clamour of voices and the roar of engines mingled with the clangour of bells and the chatter of Geiger counters. It was headlong flight and time was short.

Suddenly, without warning, the concrete walls of the two piles collapsed and deadly radiation poured out, poisoning the ground and the air. A cloud of radioactive gas rushed upward and was carried away on the wind, drifting over the land and destroying all life where it fell.

There was silence. Stonehaven became a dead place, a radioactive wasteland that could never be reclaimed.

★　★　★

Eurich was in Crispian's office when the final report came through. Both men read it in silence, then Crispian said:

'Well, Professor?'

Eurich sighed.

'It's Savage's doing. No other explanation is possible. It was at Stonehaven that he was maimed — now he's got his own back. I wish I could see where this was going to end.'

'But *how* did he do it? I thought these atomic plants had safety devices to make such a disaster impossible.'

'In normal circumstances, yes,' Eurich answered. 'But, remember, Savage has access to forces quite out of the ordinary

— and he is learning new ways to apply them all the time.'

The professor absently polished his spectacles.

'The destruction of Lima was a crude performance compared with this new outrage. Now he has some degree of control over the alien weapons — I believe that, at Stonehaven, he succeeded in altering the atomic structure of matter . . .

'He subtly changed the structure of the graphite and concrete walls until they were no longer a barrier to radiation; he also changed the structure of the cadmium safety rods so that they no longer had any effect. The uranium reaction would then continue uncontrolled, with the results we now know.'

Crispian swore, and the sound was like an explosion in that cramped room; he crossed to the window and stared out. A mist was rising, covering roofs and chimneys with a grey shroud. Where was Savage now, he wondered?

'I fear there is worse to follow,' Eurich said unhappily. 'I can't really see any way of stopping him . . . not without a full understanding of this alien science.'

Crispian did not answer. He continued to stare through the window, up to the sky and beyond, and his thoughts had nothing to do with Ralph Savage.

A spaceship had crossed the void between planets. A chill spread through his body as he considered the idea . . . suppose that were to happen again? What then?

13

Crispian in danger

Ralph Savage paced the terrace overlooking the lake, a scowl on his face and hatred in his heart. Behind him, the temple was silent except for the hum of machinery; the Incas left him alone when he was in such a mood. In one hand, he clutched a copy of a London newspaper, picked up on his travels — and, across the front page were pictures of Mary Marshall and Inspector Crispian with an announcement of their engagement.

It came as a shock. So confident had he been that both had died at Lima, that he had not bothered to search for them. And now this —

The sun blazed down on the valley and lit up the newly completed statue the Incas had erected by the edge of the water. Thirty feet high and fashioned of pure gold studded with diamonds, it

149

glittered as fiercely as the light in Savage's eyes.

He strode up and down the terrace, his disfigured face made more hideous by his ugly thoughts. Mary and Crispian! Had he not suffered enough, without this? It was an indignity not to be borne. His first thought was to destroy London as he had Lima — but he checked this impulse. He knew where to find Mary, and would bring her back — but first, Crispian must die!

And not in some general catastrophe. Savage wanted a more personal revenge . . .

He looked again at the photograph of Mary, imagining her in Crispian's arms, returning his kisses. The idea tormented him and he stalked up and down the terrace, clawing at the air with his hands and muttering to himself. A weird, surrealistic monologue began in his head and gradually escaped his lips.

'You're a fool! You had your chance and wasted it. You shouldn't have waited so long . . . *a woman respects a strong man*. You should have shown her you were master here. You offered your love and she spurned you . . . '

His obsession grew, his eyes glowed, and his demeanour became that of a madman.

'You can still have her! You must first kill Crispian, then bring her here by force . . . *kill Crispian*! Don't waste any more time, don't wait any longer. Take her now . . . '

He stopped in mid-stride, covering his face with his hands and feeling the terrible deformation with his fingertips. A cry of anguish escaped him.

'As if she could ever love you! You fool — she must turn away in horror! She could never set eyes on your face without a shudder . . . you look like . . . '

Suddenly, Savage became aware that he was talking to himself. He cursed, and turned from the terrace, striding into the hall of machines. He picked up the incendiary weapon and adjusted the setting of the alien machine that would transport him instantly to London.

He spoke once more aloud, this time deliberately.

'Crispian,' he said, 'I'm coming for you.'

Then he made a final adjustment. His gaunt figure seemed to flicker, became ghostlike, then vanished altogether.

★ ★ ★

Professor Eurich looked about him with interest as he entered Crispian's flat in Knightsbridge.

'I've always wanted to catch a policeman off duty,' he said, 'and see how he lived. A nice place you have here, Inspector.'

The room was large, with one wall entirely of glass to catch the sunlight; opposite was a divan bed. Over the writing desk hung a reproduction of a landscape by Renoir, while a long, glass-covered bookcase covered most of one wall. The furniture and decoration were in a contemporary style.

'I'll soon be looking for a house,' Crispian returned.

'Ah, yes, I heard of your engagement. Congratulations, Inspector.'

Crispian stared at the apparatus Eurich had brought with him.

'What on earth's that?' he asked.

Eurich set his apparatus upon the floor and pushed it into one corner. It was about two feet square and set on a plastic base; a network of wires protruded from a metal box, forming a complicated aerial system.

'Something, I hope, to defeat Ralph Savage,' Eurich said calmly. 'I've been hard at work the last few days — it remains only to put it to the test.'

'Well, why bring it here?'

'Really, Inspector! Do you suppose you can thwart a man like Ralph Savage and not have him after your blood? I fully expect him here with the intention of eliminating you.'

'Thanks,' Crispian said drily, 'but I'm not that important.'

'I disagree,' Eurich said. 'You took Mary Marshall away from him, and he'll be obsessed by the idea of revenging himself.'

'I'll be waiting.' Crispian stared thoughtfully at the apparatus Eurich had deposited in one corner of the room. 'What's that supposed to do?'

The professor carefully pre-set the controls of his device.

'I'll tell you about it afterwards,' he replied. 'Let's hope it works.' He took a last look round. 'Goodnight, Inspector,' he said, and left.

Crispian settled into an armchair as he listened to a recording of Beethoven's 'Pastoral' Symphony. As he listened, he read again Mary's last letter to him, then he went over to his desk and wrote in reply. A clock struck eleven and he prepared for bed. He placed Mary's photograph where he could see it when he woke — and, remembering the professor's words, loaded his revolver and put it under his pillow. Very soon, he was asleep.

* * *

Savage had no difficulty in locating Crispian's flat. As he moved, ghostlike, through deserted streets, the moon came from behind the clouds and lit his way. A clock in a jeweller's window opposite showed the time to be a little after two in the morning. He stared up at the block of flats where Crispian lived and touched the black box at his waist. Instantly, he rose in the air and faded through the wall.

He found Crispian's room. The window was open, the curtains drawn back, and a shaft of moonlight revealed the Inspector as he lay sleeping on the divan. Savage's eyes glittered when he saw his enemy helpless before him — he did not look round the room and so did not see Eurich's apparatus.

He moved a control on the black box again, bringing himself out of the inter-atomic state. He aimed his weapon and paused a moment, gloating.

'Goodbye, Inspector,' he said, and fired.

There was a blinding flash of light, followed by a smell of burning . . .

★ ★ ★

Crispian woke abruptly. After that moment of intense brightness, the room appeared as solid blackness. He turned on his side and groped under the pillow for his revolver — then he saw the shadowy figure of Ralph Savage standing over him, a look of astonishment on his face and the incendiary weapon lowered at his side.

Crispian brought up his gun and shot to kill. Savage swore, still puzzled by his enemy's escape, and touched his waistbelt. The bullet passed harmlessly through him and shattered the glass of the bookcase behind. Then, as Crispian sprang from his bed, Savage turned and vanished into the wall.

Eurich was right again, the Inspector thought — and wondered how it was he still lived. He gave thanks for that miracle, wrapped a coat round his pyjamas and ran down to the street. He saw no sign of Ralph Savage . . .

The constable on the beat reported he had seen nothing out of the ordinary and Crispian returned to his flat. He made two telephone calls, one to Scotland Yard, the other to Professor Eurich.

He sat down to wait, and became aware of a strong smell of burnt insulation. He looked at the professor's apparatus; the wires of the antenna were fused together and the whole thing seemed a ruin.

Eurich arrived by taxi twenty minutes

later and Crispian related what had happened.

'And now will you explain it all, professor? I have a feeling I shouldn't be alive if it weren't for your box of tricks.'

Eurich did not answer at once. He bent over the wreckage of his apparatus and gave it his close attention. As he straightened up, he sighed.

'A failure,' he said dejectedly.

'Not entirely,' Crispian pointed out, smiling. 'I'm still here!'

'True, Inspector, true — but I was hoping for rather more than that.' Eurich pointed to the evil-smelling mass of fused wire and metal. 'This instrument was designed to capture and retain the energy charge which Savage released. I had hoped to contain it, as a battery contains electrical energy, but obviously I underestimated the amount of power involved.

'When Savage pointed his weapon at you, and fired, the energy charge was instantly diverted to my apparatus — it was this that saved your life. Unfortunately, the insulation failed completely and the instrument was burnt out . . . with the result that I now have no sample of inter-atomic energy to experiment with. It really is most annoying!'

Crispian laughed.

'Never mind, professor, I'm sure you'll manage it next time. At least you've proved you can deflect Savage's weapon — and I'm grateful to you for saving my life. Can I offer you a drink before you leave?'

'Well, now,' Eurich said slowly, 'it's a cold night and, although I'm not a drinking man, I think perhaps I will take something. A little whisky if you have it.'

Crispian produced a bottle and two glasses from a cabinet.

'I'll join you,' he said, pouring the whisky. 'I need something myself after that.' He raised his glass. 'A toast: to the speedy downfall of Ralph Savage!'

Eurich replied: 'I was about to propose your future happiness to Miss Marshall.' He paused, looking thoughtful. 'It might be a good idea if she were to go into hiding for a while — it's only too likely that Savage will visit her next.'

14

Terror

As it happened, Mary had gone to stay with her aunt for a few days to escape the attentions of news reporters who still haunted Long Prior. So that when Savage arrived there, shaken by his failure at Crispian's flat, he was out of luck again.

He did not know quite what had happened in Knightsbridge and, suspecting a trap, did not come out of the inter-atomic state. He moved quickly through the house till he found Mary's bedroom — it was empty. He searched the rest of the house without finding her. Mr. Marshall slept quietly, unaware of his danger, and Savage left him alone — even he realized he dare not murder Mary's father.

Then, deciding to waste no more time, he returned immediately to the valley in South America. Mary Marshall could wait — she could not elude him forever . . .

But soon he had something else to think about.

Latin blood runs hot so, as soon as they recovered from the shock caused by the destruction of Lima, the Peruvians declared war on Ralph Savage. They did so with public meetings and radio broadcasts but nothing else happened for a while. Lima had been the capital, the seat of government, and now the country found itself without direction. A state of chaos ensued.

A few ministers had been away from the capital at the time of the disaster and these set about forming a new government, with Puira as their headquarters. Buildings were requisitioned and a President elected. He duly nominated his cabinet, after a series of internal crises, and plans were made to carry the war to the enemy.

Puira had been chosen partly because it had an airfield; and here gathered the strangest motley of aircraft ever seen. Fighters and bombers scrapped by a dozen nations, transport planes of obsolete vintage, one seaplane, helicopters loaned privately — anything that would fly and carry high explosives was pressed into service alongside the regular Peruvian air force. They were fuelled and loaded with bombs — all kinds of bombs, from streamlined torpedoes to homemade packages of blasting explosive.

Then, one morning at dawn, while the crowds cheered and the President made a speech that was broadcast round the world, the Peruvian air-fleet took off on its mission of retribution. It was to be an all-out attack with the intention of reducing Savage's stronghold to dust.

The massed flight of more than one hundred aircraft flew inland, across the glittering snow-clad peaks of the Andes and the verdant jungle. One or two dropped by the way, but the rest finally reached their objective. In a series of vee-formations, they swooped down on the hidden valley and unloaded their bombs. Ton after ton of high explosive was dropped . . . and not one single bomb reached its target.

Ralph Savage smiled scornfully as he watched the planes come. The Peruvians had not kept their intention secret; all the world knew, and waited. Savage waited, too.

As the first planes began to dive, he operated one of the alien machines. An inter-atomic beam shot upwards, an invisible cone of force that spread out to cover the whole sky above the valley.

The planes dived, released their bombs and flew on. Line after line of them passed, till all were gone — and not one bomb exploded anywhere near Ralph Savage. Somewhere in the air, they vanished . . .

The last plane disappeared over the horizon and Savage laughed aloud. He did not think anyone would try to bomb him again — not after the pilots returned and saw what had happened to Puira.

★ ★ ★

In Puira, the President listened by a radio for reports from his aircraft. Thousands of people lined the streets waiting for news. They were silent now, but later their voices would ring out and there would be dancing in the streets.

The sky was a deep, tropical blue and absolutely clear. Then, out of an empty sky, fell a rain of high explosive. The first angry scream of falling bombs was cut short by loud explosions. After that, there was only the noise of falling buildings and the shrieks of the dying. For thirty minutes the bombs fell and, when at last they ceased, Puira was a shambles with not one building left standing.

★　★　★

Ralph Savage was only half satisfied with his success. It had been a simple matter to catch the bombs in a cone of inter-atomic energy and transmit them to the sky above Puira. He made the attack into a boomerang, and it was the Peruvians who razed their own city.

But two things worried him; his failure to locate Mary — and the vulnerability of his own position. Both Mary and

Crispian had disappeared; gone into hiding, he guessed. Well, they could not remain hidden forever — it was only a question of time till he found them again. Meanwhile, there was this other thing; he was safe only as long as he remained in the valley to ward off attack. His weapons were entirely offensive — he needed some defensive mechanism that would operate automatically in his absence. Until he achieved that, he must remain in a state of siege.

He worked without rest to solve the problem and, eventually, had what he wanted, a machine that would throw a screen of energy over the valley. The screen took the form of a vast dome, invisible to the eye, yet impenetrable by any material substance.

And, in securing the energy screen, he discovered yet another powerful weapon in his armoury, one that would strike at the very roots of industrial civilization . . .

It was not realized, at first, what was happening in the world. Two small ships were lost with all hands. Then a mighty liner, two days out from Southampton and bound for New York, sank in mid-Atlantic. The ship went down swiftly and there were few survivors.

An enquiry was held and the one statement that all survivors agreed upon was that 'the ship seemed to fall apart.' From this, the experts deduced that some form of metal fatigue was responsible for the disaster. Authoritative assurances were given that such a thing could never happen again.

The very next day, however, a German liner plunged beneath the waves . . .

In a London suburb, a man was cleaning his motorcycle. It was not a new machine, but it had served well enough to take him and his girl to the coast on many occasions. Just now, the paintwork looked shiny and there was a clean, oily smell about it. He straightened up, both pleased and proud — and then, before his astonished eyes, the motorcycle disintegrated. In a matter of seconds, there was only a heap of dust, some flakes of paint and a spreading pool of oil.

The foreman arrived early on the site. For the past three weeks, steel girders had been climbing to the sky, the structural work for a huge block of flats. He stood regarding the site, open-mouthed. The concrete foundations lay untouched — but all the steelwork had vanished as if it never existed.

Two lovers smiled at each other over an outside table. The meal ended, he offered her a cigarette and flicked the wheel of his lighter. Then he screamed — the metal case had crumbled to dust and lighted petrol ran over his hand.

A strato-cruiser plunged to destruction; and an estate of prefabricated houses fell apart at their metal seams. On the Trans-Siberian railway, a train crashed through the side of a bridge and rolled down a mountain slope, killing twenty-seven and injuring hundreds. Subsequent inspection of the track showed that the steel rails had disintegrated.

By now, the newspapers and broadcast media were full of similar stories; every day in some cases, each new edition and bulletin brought news of such disasters. Freight insurance charges soared and travellers began to cancel bookings;

governments declared a state of emergency and commandeered all forms of transport. There was a boom in the sale of horses; and scientists performed elaborate tests on the diseased metals.

The turbines of a hydro-electrical plant collapsed, leaving a large part of Scotland without power. The giant presses used for mass-producing cars in a factory near London disintegrated and thousands of workers became unemployed. Gasometers suddenly discharged their contents into the air and oil refineries leaked highly inflammable spirit — hundreds of innocent people died in the resulting fires.

While these occurrences were serious enough, they were still isolated instances. Only a few men saw the pattern that was forming, the pattern of destruction that would inevitably lead to the breakup of civilized society. No one, so far, connected these extraordinary happenings with Ralph Savage.

The pattern was worldwide. In Paris, the Eiffel Tower shuddered and fell in powdery ruin. In New York, the steel skeleton of the Empire State building withered away and the concrete fabric crashed to the ground under its own weight.

In San Francisco, the famous Golden Gate Bridge collapsed and dropped into the sea. Right across the planet, all kinds of machines began to fail.

It seemed that no metal structure was safe, and new materials had to be found. Plastics grew in importance and machine tools became an even more vital part of industry.

Food was no longer being transported on the seas and canned goods were scarce.

As the long list of calamities increased, people of every country began to realize that the end of an era was in sight.

Panic ensued. There were riots in the cities and a feeling of terror spread as fast as the disease in iron and steel. Newspapers and commentators claimed that unless the rot was stopped, civilization would be finished.

Martial law was instigated in many lands; while, somewhere in Britain, Inspector Crispian and Professor Eurich were summoned to an emergency meeting of the Cabinet.

The polished oak table reflected a circle of grave faces. The Prime Minister's lean jaw jutted out like a rocky promontory and his eyes held the hard quality of flint.

'Gentlemen,' he said, 'the time has come for us to take drastic action. Our country is faced with ruin and there is fear in the hearts of our people. We can delay no longer.'

A growl of assent passed round the table.

'Professor Eurich, perhaps you will summarize the conclusions you have reached?'

'Certainly, sir.' Eurich rose to his feet and removed his pince-nez with a flourish. 'There is no doubt in my mind, gentlemen, that one man is responsible for the series of disasters we have suffered recently — Ralph Savage. He is insane, his mind set upon revenge, and he will most certainly succeed in wrecking our society unless he is stopped.

'With the forces at his command — forces, gentlemen, created by an *alien* science — he has evolved a technique for changing the atomic structure of metals, and in particular the structure of iron and steel on which our highly mechanized civilization is based. This structural change results in *a complete loss of tensile strength in that metal*. There is no way of combating this peril except by removing its cause — Ralph Savage.'

'Thank you, professor,' the Prime Minister said. 'It remains only to decide the method by which Savage may be eliminated.' He turned to Crispian. 'You, Inspector, have volunteered for a special mission. You have no wish to withdraw?'

'I'll do whatever's necessary,' Crispian replied.

'Good! You are the one man who has knowledge of Savage's stronghold, which is why you were asked to volunteer for this assignment.'

The Prime Minister paused, looking round the table.

'Gentlemen, I should certainly hesitate to put before you the plan I have in mind if times were normal. However, times are not normal — '

'Far from it,' interjected one of the ministers sharply.

' — and therefore I must ask that your support in this matter be in the nature of a vote of confidence. I propose that Inspector Crispian be taken as close to Savage's stronghold as is practicable in the circumstances, and that he proceed alone and secretly to this hidden valley. I propose that we commission him to kill Savage by any means whatever, and that this government should take full responsibility for his action. Do not think I am unaware of the enormity of this step, but so desperate is our situation that I believe no other course lies open to us. As Professor Eurich has said, the man is mad . . . and we must destroy him before he destroys us!'

There was complete silence around the table.

Then the Prime Minister said: 'Well, gentlemen, are you in favour of adopting my plan, or not? I beg you to remember what is at stake.'

After an uncomfortable pause, the Minister for War cleared his throat and spoke.

'There seems to be no alternative. I move that we adopt the Prime Minister's plan.'

'Seconded!'

One by one, the ministers indicated that they would support the plan to assassinate Ralph Savage.

'Very well, gentlemen.' The Prime Minister left his chair and shook Crispian by the hand. 'You have your orders, Inspector . . . good luck to you!'

Crispian left the meeting place and returned to his hideaway. It would be nice, he thought, to see Mary before he left; he hadn't seen her since they had dropped out of sight, each to a secret place in the heart of the countryside. It had been a difficult decision to separate; but that way, Savage could not strike at them both together. Now, he was eager to meet her again. His mission involved personal danger in a high degree — it might be their last meeting.

But there was bad news waiting for him when he returned to his hideaway. The phone rang steadily; and the voice at the other end was that of Mr. Marshall.

'Mary's gone,' he said grimly. 'Savage has her again!!

As Crispian replaced the receiver, he

knew that he had a strong personal motive for carrying out the government's order — he must return to that valley in South America if he were to save the girl he loved.

15

Inca Sacrifice

Crispian's plane flew through the night, due south from Panama. It was a fast military bomber, carrying only the pilot and navigator, and Crispian, flying by dead reckoning without lights.

The Inspector looked to his guns for the hundredth time to see if there were any deterioration of the metal parts, but they still seemed in good condition. He had a high-powered rifle with telescopic sights, a revolver and sheath knife; he wore a parachute and carried emergency rations, water canteen, first-aid kit and compass.

'Ten minutes to dropping point,' the navigator said casually.

Crispian nodded. His brain was clear and his nerves calm despite his excitement. He would be on his own and his mission was such that he dare not fail. He tried to keep his thoughts off Mary . . . now was no time for his reasoning powers to be coloured by emotion.

'Five minutes,' said the navigator.

Crispian checked the harness of his parachute.

'You'll have to watch your step down there,' the pilot observed. 'He has some kind of energy screen over the valley now. It's quite invisible and I don't see how you're going to get through. Still, that's your problem!'

'Stand by,' snapped the navigator.

Crispian opened the dropping hatch and stood poised. The air stream whipped past his face like a hurricane. The night was dark and ground merged into one.

'*Now* . . . '

Crispian jumped.

He fell through darkness and the plane was gone; he neither saw nor heard it again. He counted, one . . . two . . . three, and tugged sharply at the release ring. Above him, the pilot chute pulled the main silk out in a billowing cloud. He felt a mighty jerk on his harness and then he was no longer falling, but floating gently down to the invisible jungle below.

He could see nothing of the ground and the breeze swung him from side to side. He drifted down till his feet pressed on some slight obstruction; he heard the topmost branch of a tree snap under his weight. He kicked out, continuing his descent.

Other branches broke and the cords of his parachute caught up; he hung suspended — then fell through dense foliage with broad leaves slapping at his face. Finally, he caught hold of a branch and came to rest, cutting himself free of the parachute.

It was still too black to make out his surroundings, so he edged his way cautiously along the branch till he came to the main trunk. Here, in the fork of the tree, he made himself comfortable and settled to wait for daylight. Once during the night hours, he heard a wild animal near him; instinctively he grasped his revolver — and remembered he must give no warning of his approach. He shifted his grip to his knife . . . but the animal did not attack.

The dawn light showed him to be high up and about a mile east of the valley. His parachute, its silk dyed green, was almost invisible amongst the leaves so he left it there. He ate some of the concentrated food tablets and drank sparingly of his water before descending to the ground and starting the trek to the cliff edge.

By the time he cleared the jungle and saw before him the precipitous walls of the valley, the sun was high and the air hot and sticky. He stared down at the temple and saw unusual activity going on below; Incas were gathering about the thirty-foot high statue of the sun goddess. It looked as if a celebration were to take place . . . and he remembered fearfully that Mary was in Savage's power.

He approached the edge of the vertical drop — and stopped in his tracks as he saw an arc of ground burnt clear of vegetation. He had found the limit of Savage's energy screen.

Crispian threw a stone into the air — it exploded in a blinding flash of light. Another step and he would have been annihilated. He walked round the ring of charred earth, but there was no way through; the screen was continuous.

He could do nothing but wait for the barrier to go down, as he assumed it would when Savage returned — there could be no reason for him to waste power when he was present to defend his stronghold.

Crispian continued circling the valley, and selected a place to climb down when the screen was eventually removed. He rested in the shadow of trees, keeping watch on the activity below. He saw no sign of either Mary or Ralph Savage. The Indians were working themselves into a frenzy of excitement, dancing and chanting to a monotonous rhythm.

Idly, he tossed another stone towards the energy screen — and nothing happened. The stone landed intact on the ground beyond. Savage had lowered the barrier.

Crispian ran forward, heaving a sigh of relief as he passed the danger point. Then, carefully, he began the descent, lowering himself hand over hand. Though the cliff face was near vertical, it was by no means smooth; deep cracks and projecting rock afforded him hand and footholds as he slowly worked his way down.

It was an hour before he reached the bottom, then, although he felt exhausted, he did not pause to rest. He broke into a trot, making for the temple. The fields were deserted and no one challenged him. He kept the solid mass of the temple between himself and the Incas, moving up from behind, unobserved.

If his luck held, he might take Savage by surprise — and one shot could end the whole business. But even as he reached the high stone wall at the rear of the temple, a wild shout echoed from above . . .

Two Indians had spied him from the top of the steps and one threw a spear. Crispian ran along the base of the wall, cursing and unslinging his rifle. The spear missed him by a small margin and stuck in the ground.

He reached the corner of the stonework. Beyond, he saw Ralph Savage and Mary Marshall standing before the golden statue of the sun goddess. They were surrounded by Incas and so dense was the crowd that he could not get a clear shot at Savage. He looked quickly behind him; the two Indians had been joined by others and were giving chase.

He stared up at the grey stone wall; from its top he could draw a bead on Savage. He began to scale the wall, using the carved ornament like rungs of a ladder. Another spear shattered on the stone beside him. He scrambled higher with desperate speed.

He was almost to the top when a dark face peered down at him. A metal blade flashed in the sun and Crispian nearly lost his fingers; he released his hold and slid back, fumbling for his revolver. The man up top thrust down viciously with a long spear and Crispian was forced to drop to the ground.

Instantly, five Incas sprang at him. The revolver was struck from his grasp by a heavy blow that sent numbing pain shooting along his arm. He took another blow on the head and the world reeled about him. A red mist hung before his eyes. One Indian clung to his back while a second knocked his legs from under him. They went down in a heap, with Crispian still fighting.

He had to win, he just *had* to. For Mary's sake . . .

Someone jumped on his stomach, driving the air from his lungs and bringing excruciating pain; that was the end of his resistance. They took his weapons, hauled him upright and dragged him towards the crowd gathered about the glittering, golden statue.

The ranks of Incas drew back to allow them to pass and Crispian caught sight of Savage. He wore a richly-ornamented robe of blue and gold, with a golden crown upon his head. Mary, beside him, was dressed in plain white and her hands were tied behind her.

She cried out as she saw Crispian, and Savage turned, frowning at the interruption. His expression changed to one of pleasure, and then he laughed out loud.

'Well, Inspector,' he said, 'this is unexpected — but nevertheless welcome. You have arrived in time to witness my marriage to Miss Marshal, who has at last consented — '

'That's a lie,' Mary said in ringing tones. 'I tried to kill him, and failed!'

Savage ignored her.

'You shall see us married before you die, Inspector — and then my people will sacrifice you to the sun goddess.' He spoke a few words in the Inca tongue and the grey-bearded priest continued with the ceremony.

'This is a mockery,' Crispian called bitterly. 'Your ceremony doesn't mean a thing!'

The sharp point of a spear reminded him he was a prisoner, and he said no more.

The chanting voice of the high priest droned on and on; the sun beat down on the giant statue, setting its gems ablaze with colour. The lake was blue and still and beyond, against the smoking volcano, Crispian could see the leaning column of the spaceship, glittering silver in the sunlight.

It was a fantastic scene, like something out of a Hollywood film. Savage paid him no attention; Mary smiled faintly, her head high — but her face was pale and her expression desperate. Crispian had little hope for himself and bitterly regretted his failure . . . but surely Savage did not imagine that Mary would submit quietly to him? He could not watch her all the time — there would come a moment when he was offguard, and she would either slip poison in his food or a knife into his heart.

The incantation finished and the Indians dropped to their knees. Savage, his face flushed, kissed Mary on both cheeks.

'It's over,' he told her. 'You are my bride, Queen of all the Incas.'

He swung about to face Crispian, and now his dark eyes gleamed and there was an eagerness in him. This interfering policeman was going to pay for his meddling . . .

He struck Crispian in the mouth with his clenched hand.

'You've lived long enough,' he said. 'My triumph is complete. Mary is mine — and you will die!'

He rapped out a command and the Incas seized Crispian and dragged him to the base of the statue, where a solid gold block was placed in readiness for the execution. Crispian struggled helplessly. His hands were bound and he was forced to a kneeling position, with his head resting on the block. Mary looked on, horrified.

Savage stroked his beard, smiling. Everything was the way he wanted it. First Crispian, then Mary . . . he glanced sideways at her, gloating.

A tall Inca bearing a large, curved sword stepped up to Crispian. He lightly touched the Inspector's neck with the blade, gauging the stroke, then raised it high in the air. He waited for the word of command.

Savage let Crispian wait, enjoying every moment.

'You had best say your prayers, Inspector,' he cried mockingly. 'You haven't long for this world!'

Mary called out: 'Stop! Savage — spare him and I'll be everything you want . . . only let him live.'

Still the executioner waited, expression-less, his sword poised. Savage laughed, looking from the bowed figure of Crispian to the agonized face of the girl.

'Touching,' he sneered. 'She loves you, Inspector — does that mean anything to you, now?'

He spoke again in the Inca tongue, the single word of command to the executioner —

But, at that very moment, there came an unexpected diversion. The air filled with a sound like thunder and, out of the hot blue sky, fell the silver shape of a spaceship.

16

Aliens return

That moment was frozen in Crispian's memory. He twisted his head to stare up at the rapidly descending ship and the thought stabbed through his brain: *The aliens have come for the second time . . .*

He knew a great fear. *Their* weapons, in Savage's hands, had already proved too much for Earth's science to combat. Now they had returned. It could be the end of the race of Man.

The executioner let his sword fall harmlessly to the ground. The Incas seemed paralysed with fear; they stood motionless, watching the arrival of the new spaceship.

Savage was the first to act. He touched the black box at his waist and vanished instantly; then, as if released from a spell, the Indians fled, running across the fields to the shelter of the distant cliffs. Crispian and Mary alone were left to face the aliens.

Crispian got his hands to the sword lying on the ground and sawed away at his bonds. He succeeded in cutting himself free, and then released Mary. They stood together, silently watching the silver cylinder come to rest, not half a mile away from the derelict ship. When the jets cut out, there was a deafening silence, as if the very air refused to transmit the slightest sound.

Mary touched his arm and said, calmly: 'We'd better go to meet them, Arthur.'

Crispian hesitated, looking back at the temple; he supposed Savage to be there, preparing his defences.

'It's no good now,' Mary said, reading his mind. 'He'd be waiting for you — and the people in the spaceship will have the weapons to beat him. We need them on our side.'

She walked briskly towards the spaceship, and Crispian followed her.

'What makes you think they'll be friendly?' he grunted. 'They could be a bigger menace than Savage.'

'That's something we have to find out!'

Crispian felt a chill run along his spine. The ship was alien. He wondered where it had come from, and what the crew would look like. Savage had suggested that they could not be human . . .

The ship stood plumb upright, its rounded nose pointing at the sky; it towered above them, flashing silver in the sunlight. No opening showed in its smooth exterior and no one came out.

The valley was hushed. Only Crispian and Mary moved anywhere within the limits of the surrounding cliffs. They stood in the shadow of the spaceship, looking up at it.

Suddenly, there came a blinding flash of light from the direction of the temple — Savage had opened his attack. But the ship suffered no damage; a charred ring of grass appeared beyond Mary and Crispian. The aliens had set up an energy screen to protect themselves.

'Lucky for us we're inside the screen,' Crispian said tersely.

For ten minutes Savage attacked with

all the weapons at his disposal. Beams of inter-atomic force lashed the screen till it crackled and flashed with a dazzling blue light. The ground shuddered beneath them. Tremendous bolts of energy crashed into the invisible barrier and the valley was hidden from view by a violent brilliance that dazzled the eye.

Crispian held Mary in his arms and, together, they awaited the outcome of this incredible duel. If the screen failed, only for an instant, they would be annihilated . . . and, all the while, the aliens stayed inside their ship and made no attempt to retaliate.

The minutes dragged out and the fury about them mounted in intensity. There was very little sound, a subdued crackling like radio static, but the air seemed charged with electricity. There was a slight increase in temperature; but the bulk of the energy was dissipated in a pyrotechnic display so fantastic as to be almost beyond belief.

The screen held and, at last, the bombardment ceased. Savage was no longer the master; he had met his superiors.

Crispian stared towards the temple, wondering how he would take his defeat. It still remained to see what the aliens would do.

'We'd better remind them we're here,' Mary said, and began thumping on the metal hull with her clenched hands. The echo was as ponderous as a bass drum.

Time passed and nothing happened. Crispian threw himself down on the grass.

'It's up to them,' he said significantly. 'We can't even go back till they lower the energy screen.'

Mary tired of drumming on the ship's side and sat down beside him. They waited for the aliens to show themselves.

Beyond the screen, the lake was calm and the temple apparently deserted. There was no sign at all of the Indians. The sun shone down from a clear blue sky and reflected brilliantly on the golden statue. Behind the leaning column of the derelict ship, the volcano sent a dark smudge of smoke rising into the hot and windless air.

The whole valley was still.

Presently Mary whispered: 'There's a port opening above us!'

Crispian looked up. High over his head, he saw a circular opening in the silver wall and a warm, yellow light glowing within. He took a deep breath. Now for it, he thought . . . now we'll know what they look like.

But nothing happened for some minutes — then Mary gripped his arm.

'I feel funny,' she said. 'Light-headed. Do you hear anything?'

Crispian thought he heard a faint, hissing sound; and at the same time, experienced difficulty in breathing. He tried to get up and started coughing. He stumbled and fell. Mary had collapsed, her face tinged with blue, gasping for air. Crispian's lungs were pounding like bellows . . . he couldn't breathe the ground was a dark cloud swimming up at him; and then he lost consciousness.

★ ★ ★

Ralph Savage was afraid. He had tried everything he could think of to break the

191

power screen about the alien spaceship and failed. He expected a counterattack any second, and set furiously to work to save himself.

He did not stop to speculate upon the identity of the beings who had crossed the void of space; he knew only that they must be dangerous. His scientific curiosity was buried beneath an immediate and instinctive desire for self-preservation — he had to get away before the aliens turned some unknown weapon on him.

He did not think of Mary or Crispian, only of himself. But even now, he did not panic — he was not going to leave his machines behind for, without them, he would be helpless He worked feverishly, transmitting them to a new hideaway in a remote underground cavern.

When all was finished, he returned to the terrace for one last look across the valley. The ship lay dormant behind its energy shield and there was, as yet, no sign of the aliens. It astonished him that they did not attack; he would certainly not have wasted so much time . . .

Savage laughed aloud . . . they had left

it too late now. He touched the black box at his belt and vanished from the temple.

* * *

Crispian could not believe his eyes when he opened them again. What he saw was too fantastic to be taken seriously. He was either dreaming or had suffered a mental relapse. There was the lake and the temple, and the silver spaceship was exactly as it had been, and Mary lay unconscious beside him, but —

He closed his eyes and counted to ten, opened them again. The birds were still there.

They were all around him, standing three feet or more from the ground, sinister-looking birds with ebony-black bills and breast feathers of a steel-blue sheen. They had bright, beady eyes and croaked harshly one to another as they flapped about on enormous black wings. It wasn't only their size that was so terrifying; there was a cold, calculating intelligence about them.

A few stalked solemnly over the

ground, pecking at it with their sharp bills; some circled high in the air, falling and rising again on invisible air currents; others perched on the shoulders and outstretched arms of the Inca statue, their wings folded, like brooding sentinels. Altogether, there must have been about thirty of them, Crispian calculated.

Mary stirred, opening her eyes, and Crispian bent over her.

'Take it easy,' he advised. 'There's something wrong with the air. Breathe slowly and deeply till you get used to it.'

She sat up, silent with wonder as she saw the birds. The larger specimens had a wing-span of six feet and the flight feathers were tinted with a purple iridescence: long throat hackles projected from beneath the heavy bills.

'So these are the — visitors from another world,' she said. 'Crows, giant crows!'

'They're more like ravens,' Crispian observed.

Mary shuddered. 'They *do* look sinister . . . '

The aliens, seeing that Crispian and Mary had recovered, gathered round them in a flock. They stared intently at the two humans, cawing their raucous notes.

Crispian said, helplessly: 'I don't see how we're ever going to communicate.'

Mary walked up boldly to the nearest bird and began stroking its feathers just behind the head; she talked quietly to it, trying to show that she wanted to be friends, as she would with any of Earth's feathered creatures. The outsized raven cawed a softer note and lowered its head on her shoulder.

Then Crispian overcame his fear sufficiently to stroke another of the aliens. It had a strong body odour that was not unpleasant.

'Strange to think that these creatures have crossed space,' he mused. 'They don't look like super-technicians, yet that's what they must be to have built this ship. I wonder where they come from?'

'Let's hope they're as bright at communications,' Mary said. 'We've got to make them understand we need help against Savage — after all, it's their weapons he's using.'

She picked up a stone and began to

scratch simple symbols in the soft earth.

'We'll start with mathematics, Arthur, because that's supposed to be a universal language. A circle is still a circle and a triangle a triangle, wherever their home is.'

She drew a circle to represent the sun; moved off and made a small dot to indicate Mercury, the planet nearest the sun; further out still for Venus, Earth and Mars — she continued through the outer planets.

'There,' she exclaimed, 'that's the solar system — they *must* recognize that!'

She stood beside the small circle marking Earth and looked hopefully at the birds. They had watched closely, and now, spread their wings and rose into the air.

'It's hopeless,' Crispian said. 'There's no common basis to work on.'

One by one, the birds flew into the spaceship; the last of them perched on the edge of the circular opening, looking down.

'Obviously, they expect us to follow,' Mary said calmly.

'Flying is natural to them, and probably they think our arms act as wings.'

'Pity they don't,' Crispian remarked, and began to jump about, flapping his arms in a pantomime intended to convey to the aliens his lack of flying ability.

Mary watched him wide-eyed. The sight of a six-foot man with red hair hopping around like a schoolboy was too much for her. She giggled.

'Really, Arthur — you haven't the build for a ballet dancer.'

He stopped and glared at her.

'Well, you think of something . . . '

They waited expectantly for the alien reaction. The minutes passed slowly.

'They might at least throw down a rope,' Crispian growled. 'Not that I'm keen to step inside that thing.'

He remembered Savage's comment about the absence of any ladderway to enable the crew to move about; that was explained now — wings were just as effective inside the ship as out.

Then, silently, another port opened in the side of the vessel, this time at ground level.

'We're not doing so bad,' Mary said. 'They understood that, all right.'

She moved forward to enter the ship, but Crispian grabbed her.

'Not so fast,' he said grimly. 'We don't know what we may be walking into.'

'We must take the risk, Arthur. No one else can help us stop Savage.'

She shook off his hand and climbed into the opening and Crispian followed her.

17

The Talking machine

Crispian stood at the bottom of an immense shaft, looking up past rows of bizarre machines, each a variation of the basic shell-whorl form. The air glowed with a soft, yellow radiance and a chorus of harsh cries emanated from the raven-like birds perched at various levels above him. The central thoroughfare of the spaceship stretched emptily upward, tapering away to a tiny ring of light at its apex.

As he watched, the aliens lowered a sphere towards him. It was about two yards across, with a pearly sheen, and came to rest on a level with his eyes. He heard a small humming sound and the pearly sheen began to change; it became translucent and he could see into the sphere.

What he saw there was an image. The

picture was indistinct at the edges and changed steadily; it showed an alien landscape, as if a low-flying craft were passing over the scene and recording it.

He saw a limitless expanse of desert, rust-red and ochre coloured. The sky was tinged with blue and faint wisps of cloud drifted across it. So clear was the image that, for a moment Crispian thought he could have stepped on to that reddish sand; he could almost sense the thinness of the atmosphere and feel the cold chill of it seep into his bones.

The desert was monotonously flat, with only here and there a range of low hills or an outcrop of eroded rock. There were deep vee-shaped grooves cut across the planet with geometrical precision, an intricate network of them, and pale green vegetation growing on the gently sloping banks.

'It's an old world,' Mary said excitedly. 'It reminds me somewhat of the old mistaken conceptions of Mars. I think I can even see canals!'

The scene changed slowly and they saw the polar ice-caps, melting under the direct rays of the sun to send a torrent of water pouring through the artificial channels that irrigated the land.

A dust storm swept across the surface of the planet, a solid wall of driven sand that temporarily blotted out the view. The image was so realistic that Crispian found himself holding his breath as that terrifying wall rushed towards him.

The storm passed, and now he had a distant view of the planet, with the curvature of the horizon quite distinct and three moons hanging in the sky. Giant ravens wheeled in flocks over the desert, sometimes diving to feed on the canal plants.

Crispian saw tall obelisks inscribed with strange hieroglyphs, and a blood-red pyramid surrounded by majestic monoliths; in contrast, odd pieces of statuary were scattered at random across the planet. Fantastic arabesques of metal sprouted from the labyrinthine hollows in lumps of rock, reminding him of some modern sculpture he had seen. The aliens used these startling constructions as perches — it seemed they had a practical use for sculpture.

Presently, the vision faded and the sphere assumed again its pearly opalescence.

'Well,' Mary said, drawing a deep breath. 'Well . . . '

Crispian, too, felt at a loss for words.

The aliens removed the sphere, raising it to one of the higher levels of the ship, and replaced it by a machine of their usual shell-like variety. This one was larger than any of the machines Savage had transferred to the temple and pulsed like a living body, expanding and contracting, humming all the while.

It did not seem to be doing anything till Crispian reached out his hand and touched it. Then a mechanical voice said:

'We, of Karz — '

He stepped back in surprise and the voice cut off.

'English,' he said, stupefied. 'It spoke in English — a machine!'

Mary was quick to realize that the machine had stopped because Crispian had withdrawn his hand. She let her fingers rest lightly on the spiral casing.

'We, of Karz,' continued the mechanical voice, 'greet you the people of Earth. We have travelled from the solar system of the star you call Vega, some 26 light years distant.'

'Welcome to Earth,' Mary replied promptly. 'We are glad you have returned and seek your help. We wish to be friends.'

'We, of Karz, thank you,' said the machine. 'We hope this meeting will benefit both races. Though we are of different origins and have different cultures, the common factor of intelligence should overcome all differences.' It paused. 'You may ask questions.'

Crispian laid his hand on the machine. It seemed to throb under his touch and he felt as if part of him were drawn into it in some mysterious way.

'What I want to know is,' he said, 'how can you speak our language?'

'We cannot,' came the answer. 'The machine translates for us.'

'How?'

'All speech is basically a matter of sound waves travelling through an atmosphere and the pattern of waves is related to thoughts in the brain. When you touch the machine you provide a material link; the machine taps your nervous system and achieves contact with the brain cells. It is thus able to relate language to thought. The machine picks up the pattern of your sound waves, correlates them to the idea in your brain, then translates that idea into the Karzian language. It also works in reverse so that you may understand us.'

'That's wonderful!' Mary exclaimed.

'Why did you put us to sleep?' Crispian demanded.

'That was an accident. We were careless in allowing our air supply to mix with your atmosphere. On Karz, although the atmosphere is similar in composition to your own, its density is considerably less. We are able to exist side by side now, because we have achieved a balance between the two. We apologize for the inconvenience.'

Yeah, Crispian thought, *that's fine — but you're still alien and I'm not sure how far I can trust you.*

'Are you the only form of life on Karz?'

Mary asked. 'I didn't see any animals — other birds, even.'

'Yes, we are alone now. Some thousands of years ago, there were other, lower forms of life on Karz, but as the planet aged, the land turned to dust and our water dwindled, it became a fight for survival. We alone, the dominant species, survived by our mastery of inter-atomic forces.'

Mary looked thoughtful.

'I suppose you must have visited other worlds than Earth?'

'Yes, but intelligent life exists only on Karz, Earth and Vorga, a planet in our own system. We are the most highly developed race; you are steadily growing towards maturity; the Vorgans are still primitive. No other planet in either solar system supports intelligent life in any recognizable form — and so far we have not encountered intelligent life in the other systems we have explored.'

'Vorga — what's that like?'

'Vorga is a strange world indeed, a planet isolated by dense cloud. There is no direct sunlight at all, merely a dull blue glow that seeps through the twilight gloom. Consequently, the inhabitants have no conception of our solar system, no science of astronomy, no idea of the vast numbers of stars that exist throughout the universe. Their world is bounded by a hazy sky, an impenetrable mist . . .

'For them, Vorga is the entire universe! The land is arid for there is no water at all on Vorga; where once oceans existed, there are now dust bowls. The soil is a bright yellow and very hot; the atmosphere — mainly carbon dioxide — is also heated to a high temperature. The whole planet is hot . . .

'Vegetation cannot grow there and the landscape is utterly bleak and surrounded by perpetual mist. It is not surprising, therefore, that the Vorgans have progressed little. Their life is a continual struggle for survival. They live like animals, in burrows underground, grubbing for food and procreating the race; their intelligence is no more than natural cunning in the face of a hostile environment.'

Mary shivered. Earth, it seemed, was a

paradise compared to both Vorga and Karza.

Crispian stared up at the sombre figures perched above him and, with his hand still on the translation machine, asked bluntly:

'Are you proposing to colonize Earth?'

'No. We are, not unnaturally, attached to our own world — we prefer to remain on Karza, even though the environment deteriorates year by year. We have no intention of making a mass exodus to your planet. You have nothing to fear from us.'

I wonder, Crispian thought grimly. *Earth must look pretty good to you* . . .

'One of your spaceships landed here before,' he said. 'It was full of weapons.'

'Weapons? All our machines serve a double purpose. It depends how they are used. If you have found only weapons, it is because you have used them destructively.'

'We need your help against the person using them,' Mary said quickly. 'Already he has killed thousands of our people and will destroy our civilization unless he is prevented.'

'There are *two* intelligent races on Earth?'

'No. But Savage — that's the man who found your ship — is insane. He wishes only to destroy.'

There was a pause.

'We do not understand. Surely you do not mean that you are using the machines against yourselves?'

'One of our race is — he is mad. Will you help us?'

Again there was a pause.

'We still do not understand.'

Crispian sighed.

'It was Savage who attacked this ship just now,' he explained patiently. 'With your own weapons. I am a police officer — if that means anything to you — and my orders are to kill Savage.'

'Kill one of your own kind?' Even through the mechanical translator, the Karzians' astonishment was apparent.

'Yes,' Crispian retorted. 'Is that so strange? After all, this is a matter of life or death for us. What would you do if a Karzian ran amok?'

'No Karzian could kill another of his

208

kind. It is impossible. We would use our weapons only against another race seeking to destroy us — to use them against ourselves is unthinkable. That would be race suicide!'

This isn't getting us anywhere, Crispian thought. How could he make them understand? He turned to the girl.

'Mary — ' he began.

But his words were lost in the noisy violence of an explosion. The spaceship shuddered, swaying dangerously as the ground shifted under it. Both Crispian and Mary were flung across the room, and lost contact with the translation machine. Beyond the still-open port, the valley was bathed in a fiery glow . . . the volcano had erupted.

Abruptly, sound and vision cut off as the port closed. There was a moment's silence before the rockets fired, and then the ship rose into the air.

Crispian held on to Mary as sudden pressure clamped them to the floor. It did not last many seconds. The ship stopped accelerating and levelled off.

Crispian sat up, dazed. 'What happened?'

'That was Savage again,' Mary said bitterly. 'He's destroyed the valley as he did Lima. He used the inter-atomic weapon to create an artificial earthquake!'

A metal panel slid back in the spaceship's hull, revealing a transparent porthole through which they could see the holocaust below. For a time, clouds of smoke and steam obliterated the view, then, as the gloom cleared, the valley became visible once more. The ground rose up and fell away and molten lava made fiery rivers, burning a path across the now unrecognizable landscape. The cliff walls had vanished as if they never existed and the jungle blazed furiously.

The temple had gone, and the lake, and the golden statue . . . even as they watched, the earth yawned again and spewed forth liquid magma. Incandescent rocks were thrown high into the air. It was like looking into the mouth of Hell . . .

Mary turned away, shaking, her face ashen.

'The Incas,' she said. 'They're down there somewhere.'

'Another crime for which Savage must

'pay.' Crispian stared into the inferno. Nothing could live there. Nothing.

'It was a quick death,' he said. 'They wouldn't feel much — though they deserved better than that. Anyway, it's over now.'

Mary swung about to face the Karzians.

'Perhaps, now,' she said quietly, 'you will help us . . . '

18

Conference

The Karzian spaceship moved at a leisurely pace over the jungle, travelling eastwards. It showed no sign of making another landing.

Crispian tired of watching the view from the port and turned away.

'Well,' he said. 'One thing is certain — Savage shifted his headquarters before he destroyed the valley. Now we've got to start looking for him all over again.'

Mary stared wistfully at the giant ravens.

'If only we could make them understand. They could stop Savage if they wanted to.'

'If . . . they're *alien*, remember. Their values are different to ours.'

Mary walked across to the translation machine and laid a hand on it.

'Savage just tried to kill you,' she said flatly. 'You can understand that, all right.

And he's not one of you. Now will you help us?'

'We hesitate to interfere in human affairs,' came the prompt reply. 'We should need a great deal more information before we commit ourselves. In any case, our force screen is sufficient protection against the inter-atomic machines.'

That's fine, Crispian thought, *you're all right — but what about us?*

He joined Mary by the translation machine, and touched the intricate metal whorls. Again he had the sensation of being linked to it.

'You have already interfered in our affairs,' he said bluntly. 'You supplied the weapons Savage is using. The least you can do is to give us similar weapons with which to defend ourselves.'

There was a pause. Crispian found himself wondering which of the Karzians was conducting the conversation; they did not appear to need physical contact with their machine and so he had no way of knowing.

'We left our original ship here many centuries ago. We thought that when you had mastered inter-atomic energy, then you would be ready for interstellar communications. Within our vessel was a detector, linked to an ultra-wave transmitter. When inter-atomic forces had been released on Earth, a faster than light message was transmitted back to our home world.

'So we came back to Earth for the second time, our ship able to travel faster than light by foreshortening space. Now, we are not sure . . . it is hardly intelligent to use such weapons against yourselves!'

'I've told you,' Crispian said. 'Savage is insane! You might at least take back your machines and leave us in peace.'

'That is being considered.'

'Perhaps you would be willing to meet representatives of our government?' Mary suggested. 'They might convince you of the urgency of the matter.'

'We are willing to meet them.'

'Good.' Crispian produced pencil and paper from his pocket and drew a rough map of Europe. He pointed to the south of England. 'Here,' he said. 'Put us down here.'

It was raining on Salisbury Plain. Under a grey, overcast sky, rain lashed the ancient stone circle where once Druids had worshipped. Further off, the town of Amesbury was just visible behind the silvery column of the Karzian spaceship.

Crispian stood bare-headed and dry under the vast dome of the energy screen, waiting for the conference to begin. He felt out of place amongst so many politicians and high officials. Mary and Professor Eurich were with him, and the three of them stood behind the ring of statesmen seated about the translation machine. This had now been fitted with tentacular extensions to cope with the number of people joining in the first interplanetary conference.

Three Karzians were perched on metal rods projecting from the machine, while others flew in lazy circles overhead. The atmosphere under the screen had been slowly adapted for both human and Karzian participants.

It had taken three days to make all the

arrangements and the elite of the political world were present. The Prime Minister and Foreign Secretary represented Britain; the Presidents of France and the United States their respective countries; Russia and China had sent two delegates from their Central Executive Committees; and the Secretary-General of the United Nations had been invited to act as chairman.

Besides these, there were members of a dozen smaller nations, scientists and military men. Newspaper reporters and television recording units were present. Armed guards and intelligence agents cordoned the whole area.

It was a unique gathering for a unique occasion.

Standing at the back, Mary said despondently: 'I've a feeling this is going to degenerate into a political wrangle. Have you noticed how everyone has accepted the Karzians, their ship and the energy screen, almost as if they had always been on Salisbury Plain. Each country wants the secrets of inter-atomic energy for itself. If they're not careful, even Savage is going to get pushed into the background in the rush to grab what they can.'

Crispian merely grunted; the same idea had occurred to him — and he didn't think the Karzians would be impressed.

The conference began quietly with an address by the Secretary-General. After a brief welcome, he plunged into the main business.

'We, the peoples of Earth, appeal to you for help. Ralph Savage, with the aid of your science of inter-atomic forces, is threatening to destroy our civilization. He has taken vast quantities of gold, the basis of our economic life, from our treasuries. He has destroyed the city of Lima and two smaller towns, murdering the inhabitants. Now he is subtly changing the structure of our metals so that iron and steel disintegrate and our ships sink and buildings fall part. This failure of our metals is like a disease spreading across the planet . . . and all this because Savage imagines society is to blame for an accident that distorted his face. Certainly it distorted his mind — the man is obviously insane!

'He must be stopped before it is too late to rebuild our civilization. Our own weapons, even the cobalt bomb, are useless against the impenetrable defence of the energy screen, and so we appeal to you — '

'If you will give us inter-atomic weapons,' cut in the United States delegate, 'we can deal with Savage ourselves.'

There was an instant hubbub of voices raised in protest; voices speaking German, Japanese, Spanish and Hindustani.

One of the Russians cried out: 'The weapons must be given to all nations, not only to the capitalist dictators of the western world!'

'Why do you speak with many tongues?' inquired the mechanical voice of the translation machine. 'Why are you divided against yourselves?'

The Secretary-General called for order, but he did not attempt to answer the Karzians' questions.

'It would be best,' he suggested. 'if the weapons were made available to a select committee of the United Nations — a

218

committee composed of representatives of all the major powers.'

'And if we gave you these machines, would you not use them against each other?'

They're learning fast, Crispian thought. *We're not going to get much help from the Karzians.*

'We only want them to stop Savage wrecking our world,' someone protested.

'And what would you do to Savage? Kill him?'

There was the faintest hint of disapproval of the mechanical voice.

Britain's Prime Minister answered sternly: 'He has murdered and must stand trial — that is our law. The people will demand that he be punished for his crimes.'

'The one man who has discovered how to operate our inter-atomic machines? Perhaps he is the more intelligent, after all . . . '

The conference dissolved in an uproar and it was several minutes before the Secretary-General could command attention. But then it was too late. The

Karzians had the last word.

'We have heard your side of the affair . . . now we must hear what Savage has to say. We shall let you know our decision in due course.'

One by one, the giant ravens flew into their ship. The translation machine was removed and the energy screen switched off. Then, as the delegates dispersed, the spaceship rose into the clouds and disappeared from sight.

★   ★   ★

Crispian and Mary were back in London after the conference. Both felt there was no immediate danger to themselves now that Savage had gone into hiding; and they were eager to find a house where they could live when they married.

It was an unfamiliar London they returned to; all manner of public services had broken down — and there was no pattern to it. They ate at an exclusive restaurant, by candlelight; and drove back to Crispian's flat in a horse-drawn carriage. Yet the radio and television still operated and newspapers came out.

They sat drinking sherry, not quite relaxed — not with the evidence of a falling civilization all about them. There were questions without answer: where was Savage now? Would the Karzians agree to stop him? It was a time of waiting, of suspense.

Outside, a newsboy shouted:

'Special edition . . . report on the Karzian conference . . . special!'

Crispian ran down to buy a copy, and Mary's face, when she read the headlines, showed disgust.

'Must they print stuff like this, Arthur? Listen —

KARZIANS REFUSE TO STOP SAVAGE!
Monster Ravens Condemn Earth!
From our Political Correspondent:
Salisbury, Tuesday.

The first interplanetary conference, from which so much was expected, revealed only that we shall get no help from the Karzian invaders who have put their terror weapons at the disposal of madman Ralph Savage! Hard on this startling revelation, a world-famous scientist gave it as his opinion that this is the first part of a plan for the Karzians conquest of Earth. With their own planet unable to support them, the sinister *passerines* of Karz see Earth as a paradise to be exploited for their own purposes. We are on the verge of interstellar war . . . '

Mary threw down the paper and snapped:

'There's more of it in the same vein. I've never read such rubbish — it's a complete distortion of what actually happened. I wish, now, that I'd never suggested the meeting in the first place!'

'You mustn't blame yourself,' Crispian said mildly. 'It's not your fault. Politicians being what they are. I suppose we might have foreseen something like this. We were a little naive, that's all. Anyway, the papers will print anything for a sensation — I shouldn't take too much notice of it.'

Mary stamped her foot to show her annoyance.

'But what will the Karzians think?'

Crispian shrugged.

'I don't suppose they'll ever see it, so it doesn't really matter. The important thing is — '

He broke off, trying to imagine the coming meeting between the Karzians and Savage.

'The important thing is . . . what are they going to make of Ralph Savage?'

19

Underground

Deep under the Pyrenees, the range of mountains that divides France from Spain, Ralph Savage had his hideaway. Inaccessible by normal means, he felt safe enough . . . except from the aliens who had so unexpectedly arrived on Earth. Here, in a vast cavern hundreds of feet below ground, he waited in fear.

The first few hours he spent in utter darkness, shivering with cold. He did not use any of his machines for fear of detection; then, in a moment of rage, he transported a small stone to the solid rock under that distant South American valley, and removed it from its inter-atomic state. The resulting catastrophe wiped out the valley completely.

Again he waited in darkness. A sense of aloneness pervaded his being and his thoughts turned to Mary. He had been a

224

fool not to bring her with him . . .

He could not remain long without heat or food, and so he was forced to use one of the machines on a low power rating. He lit the underground cavern that was to be his new home, and saw fantastic stalagmites rising from the floor. A narrow tunnel ended in an icy-cold stream that trickled through the rock; the air was dank, with an earthy tang to it. Faint marks on the walls indicated that prehistoric man had made his home here long ago.

He made brief foraging raids outside to get food, and learnt that the alien spaceship had landed in England. He wondered about that, but still did not use the energy screen; by restricting his use of power to a minimum he might yet escape detection. He paced restlessly between his silent machines, the need for action growing within him He did not enjoy being forced to hide like a common criminal. He touched his face with his fingertips and thought of Stonehaven . . . Stonehaven no longer existed. He wanted now to destroy every vestige of the society that had made him an outcast. He wanted —

Savage stopped in mid-stride and sniffed the air. It had changed subtly; he found difficulty in breathing. Had the air supply to the cavern been blocked by a fall of rock? Or —

Had the aliens found him?

He touched the black box at his waist and entered the inter-atomic state. He was perfectly calm, his feeling one of scientific curiosity. Was he about to meet the creators of the strange machines he had taken for his own?

An opalescent sphere came floating through the rock wall to hang suspended in the air before his eyes. As he watched, the sphere became translucent and he could see an image forming inside it. He saw an alien landscape, a desert of reddish sand cut across by deep, vee-shaped channels . . .

Karz, thought Ralph Savage, and watched closely. His fear had gone completely. If the aliens had intended to attack, they would not indulge in a picture-show first. Obviously, they wanted to communicate.

The view in the sphere changed constantly. He saw a series of low dunes; and watched as the wind lifted the dust and drove it across the surface, levelling one dune to build another, elsewhere. The process was continuous while the wind held. The only water lay at the bottom of the artificial canals, the only plant life grew along their banks. Karz was a bleak and desolate world.

Then he saw the Karzians —

Giant birds circled slowly on jet-black wings, turning, rising and falling on the wind currents. Their movements were almost invariably based upon a spiral and this, he guessed accounted for the form of their machines. He studied them closely and noted the heavy bill, the steel-blue sheen of the breast feathers; dark and sombre the birds appeared against the rust-coloured desert.

'Allied to the raven family,' Savage muttered.

A dying world . . . It occurred to him that Earth must look very pleasant to the Karzians. Perhaps they intended to settle here; if so, he could be of inestimable help to them — and he felt no loyalty to his own people. They would aid in destroying the society he loathed.

The sphere clouded over and the vision faded.

A harsh cry from behind made him turn quickly. One of the Karzians had materialized through the rock while his attention had been held. It hovered in the air above a shell-like machine, the casing of which pulsed rhythmically.

The giant raven closed its wings and dropped to the ground close to Savage — and he saw that it was no longer in the inter-atomic state necessary to penetrate the rock above. It regarded him with bright, beady eyes and extended a claw to touch the new machine. It did this three times and then Savage understood what was required of him.

His fingers closed on the black box at his waist and his body again assumed material substance. Then he laid his hand on the curiously pulsating skin of the Karzian machine; instantly he felt as if part of him were drawn into it. 'You are

228

Ralph Savage?' enquired a mechanical voice. 'The man who discovered our first spaceship and learnt to operate our inter-atomic machines?'

Savage was startled, but he managed to retain control of himself.

'I am,' he answered calmly. 'I alone of the peoples of Earth have solved the secrets of your weapons.'

'Certain members of your race seek to kill you — '

Savage interrupted, laughing.

'I know it — and they can do nothing!'

'You have been accused of destroying Earth's cities and murdering the inhabitants. We have come to hear your account of these events before we take action. You may speak.'

Cunning made Savage wary — he must be careful not to antagonize these powerful beings.

'I had to defend myself,' he said boldly. 'You can see what they've done to me . . . look at my face! I served my country in an atomic power plant — not the subtle process you have evolved, but a crude and dangerous release of energy where radiation is given off. I was exposed to that radiation. Now I want revenge.'

'Our machines can be used constructively, yet you saw only weapons in them. Why didn't you use the inter-atomic forces for the good of your race? Isn't it obvious that in struggling amongst yourselves, you only ensure the extinction of your species?'

'You'd like that,' Savage said sharply. 'Then you could take over Earth! Well, I'll help you — '

'We have no desire to leave Karz. It is strange — you seem intelligent, yet you wish to destroy. Why did you destroy the valley where our ship landed?'

'That was an accident,' Savage lied. The machine remained silent and he grew apprehensive. 'What do you intend doing?' he asked.

'We have no wish to harm you, or to interfere in human affairs. We came to Earth because we thought you were ready for contact with another intelligent race. We wish only an exchange of information . . . now we have doubts of the wisdom of remaining here. There are many things we do not understand.'

Again the machine lapsed into silence. Savage waited uneasily.

'Perhaps you are not entirely to blame,' declared the Karzian at last. 'Every individual is conditioned by the society in which he lives. We did not anticipate that you would use our machines only for purposes of self-destruction — the implications of that are disturbing.'

Fear returned to Ralph Savage, and he asked again: 'What are you going to do?'

'You need not be afraid of us. We shall withdraw now, to consider what must be done.'

The sphere had already been removed from the cavern; now the translation machine disappeared. As Savage watched, the Karzian spread black wings and soared upwards, vanishing through the solid roof of rock.

Alone once more, Savage became the prey of his own fears. He did not trust the Karzians; there were many things he had to do, but first he must get away. Underground, he felt cut off and at their mercy. He must find a new base for his operations.

★ ★ ★

The Karzian spaceship glided effortlessly through the clouds above a patchwork of blue and green that was so unlike the world from which it came. Earth was full of interest for the Karzians — yet oddly repulsive.

A lush world, teeming with life, rich in vegetation and with a plentiful supply of water. There was much to envy — and yet, strangely, they felt no desire to remain.

In their own language, the Karzians debated what action they were to take.

'The situation is entirely without parallel in our experience,' observed an elder. 'At no time in our history have we attacked one another. And, even if we were to deal with the man, Savage, I doubt that the situation would be greatly changed — other men would use our science of inter-atomic forces for destruction.'

'True — these Earthlings seem possessed of intelligence, without the necessary counter-balance of wisdom.'

'Then would it not be best to withdraw completely?' suggested one bird with a magnificent crest. 'In my opinion, it was a mistake to visit Earth at all! No good can come of contact with so uncivilized a race.'

'But then,' objected another, 'we should be leaving our machines in the hands of those unfitted to operate them. If the race of man were to annihilate itself utterly, we should be to blame. The extinction of an entire species is a heavy burden to carry.'

'It is against our policy to interfere — '

'Normally, but remember — if we had not landed here and left our machines, this situation could not have arisen. I feel that we must rectify matters as far as we can.'

'But what can we do? Even we have nothing superior to the energy screen, and if Savage surrounds himself with the screen, then we are helpless.'

'That is so. But Savage intends to

continue with his plan of destruction
— his attitude was made quite clear at
our meeting with him — and he cannot
do that from behind the screen. He must
lower it sometime.'

'Very well — but after we have taken
the weapons from him, what will happen
to him then? He, too, would not be in the
position he is, if we had not left the ship.
Are we simply to leave him to his fate?'

The spaceship circled leisurely above
the sea, a silver cylinder glinting in the
sun. Observers watched it through tele-
scopes and the whole world waited for the
outcome.

'The people of Earth would kill him
— that is quite obvious.'

'Perhaps we could help him? It is clear
that he needs treatment.'

'Perhaps. But not on Earth.'

'No, not here . . . '

There was a pause in the discussion
while the Karzians considered this new
aspect of the problem; then the elder
asked:

'We shall withdraw then, taking our
machines with us? Is that agreed?'

There was a general assent.

'Yes . . . it is agreed.'

'One final point. We shall need help. The man, Crispian, I think?'

'Yes, the man, Crispian, is entirely suitable.'

The nose of the spaceship dipped and the vessel slanted down to land.

20

Disaster

'It's a lovely old house,' Mary said dreamily, 'and I'm set on having it. We can, can't we, Arthur?'

Crispian sighed, and protested:

'But a Detective Inspector's salary isn't all that large.'

They had been house-hunting again, for the wedding was to be next month, and the white-stone building in St. John's Square had captured Mary's heart. Well-proportioned, it overlooked tree-shaded gardens — a peaceful haven in the very centre of busy London.

'You're forgetting that I won the World Beauty Contest in Los Angeles,' Mary retorted. 'With my prize money as a deposit, the remaining mortgage will be quite manageable. I'm serious, Arthur — I've fallen in love with the place and am determined to have it.'

Crispian shrugged.

'Then I suppose that settles it!'

It was a rambling building with large rooms and a staircase that curved up from the hall to the upper storey. Crispian liked it well enough — he had already earmarked his den — but the price would have been too high for his salary alone.

'A splendid garden at the back,' Mary said. 'I hope you like gardening, Arthur?'

'A fine kitchen, too — I hope you can cook!'

They moved from room to room and, suddenly, Mary stopped and turned to face Crispian.

'This,' she announced firmly, 'will be the nursery.'

Crispian began to say something about counting chickens, and changed his mind — the remark seemed a little too personal.

They went downstairs again.

'Well,' Mary said. 'Is it settled?'

'You're the one with the money . . . '

'Then it is settled. I'll start taking measurements for the curtains now.'

From St. John's Square, they went

directly to Mary's solicitor, and she instructed him to buy the house on her behalf.

'I'll be the envy of the department,' Crispian said. 'I doubt if even the Commissioner could afford anything like that.'

'That just shows how clever you are, darling, to marry a wealthy woman!'

When they returned to Crispian's flat, the telephone was ringing. The Inspector picked up the receiver and an official voice announced that the Commissioner wanted a word with him. There was a moment's pause.

'Crispian, get out to Salisbury as fast as you can. The Karzians want you. I gather this is it — they're willing to co-operate and insist on having you along. You know your orders . . . good luck!'

Crispian put down the telephone and looked at Mary. She only smiled, and said:

'I'm coming, too.'

He nodded; Mary, he had learnt, was a girl used to having her own way — but he made a mental note to change that after they were married.

Getting to Salisbury was not easy. The train service had been discontinued shortly after Savage had begun using the weapon that destroyed the tensile strength of iron, and the roads were littered with the debris of cars. They were forced to make many detours to avoid the ruins of fallen buildings, and the countryside was quieter than Crispian could ever remember it. Horses were replacing tractors and no planes roared overhead.

They reached Salisbury Plain eventually and headed for the glittering, silver column that was the Karzian spaceship. The energy screen was not up, but a military cordon kept back the crowds who had come out of curiosity.

An Intelligence captain checked Crispian's credentials before passing him.

'Rather you than me, Inspector,' he said bleakly. 'I don't trust these Karzians.'

A ragged cheer rose from the crowd as Crispian and Mary approached the ship. Several of the Karzians were circling overhead, their black feathers and bead-like eyes giving them a sinister aspect.

Mary shivered, and said: 'We mustn't judge by appearances, Arthur. Because we consider the raven a bird of ill-omen, that doesn't mean the Karzians wish us harm. They can't help the way they look, and anyway, it's only a superstition.'

'But they're still *alien*,' Crispian replied, 'and we don't really know much about them. Let's hope this offer of help is genuine.'

They were close to the spaceship now and a port near the ground opened for them. They entered, the Karzians flew in behind them and the port closed. The rockets fired and the ship rose on mighty jets and headed out to sea.

'What now?' Crispian wondered, and laid his hand on the translating machine.

'We are glad you have come,' the Karzians said. 'We have talked with the man Savage and agree that he must be prevented from carrying out his plans of destruction. We intend to take our machines from him before returning to our own planet — then all contact between Earth and Karz must cease. You are not yet ready for interstellar relations.'

'How can we help?' Crispian asked.

'Your minds work on a different level from our own — you will know better what to expect from Savage.'

'Where is he now?' Mary said.

'We left him in an underground cavern, but our detectors tell us he has since moved to an island in the Pacific Ocean. It remains to be seen whether he will stay there or attempt to hide elsewhere. In either case we shall eventually trace him.'

'And then?' Crispian asked.

'It will not be easy. We have no weapon superior to the energy screen, and must wait our opportunity to capture Savage.'

'You won't take him without a fight,' Crispian said bluntly. 'You'll have to kill him in the end.'

'We don't want to do that. He has a sick mind, and that can be cured by suitable treatment.'

Crispian doubted it, but said nothing — so long as Savage was stopped, the method was immaterial to him.

The spaceship sped above a strangely deserted sea; no ships plied the Atlantic now, and the air was clear of aircraft. The

241

breakdown of iron and steel had effectively killed any desire for travel. Below, there was an unbroken vista of blue-green until the eastern coastline of the United States was reached — then a few small sailing boats could be seen.

Baltimore had been hard hit; the harbours were jammed with the crumbling hulks of ocean liners; the railroad was deserted, and a solitary car travelling one of the broad avenues that led out of the city seemed like a relic from a bygone age.

For an hour, the spaceship flew over the vast wheat fields of the mid-western states, an endless blaze of tawny-yellow. In places, the railroad track had completely disintegrated and they saw the wreck of a train that had plunged through a weakened bridge. They crossed the Grand Canyon, a great grey crack in the land, and reached the Pacific coast.

'That's Los Angeles,' Mary said, pointing to the distance. 'If I hadn't gone there, we might never have met.'

The spaceship left land behind and pursued a southwesterly course, losing height and speed. Several small islands showed in the glittering water below.

Crispian touched the translation machine once more

'Have you located Savage?' he asked.

'Our detectors have picked up traces of inter-atomic energy. Watch the island with three palms on the headland.'

The ship descended through cloud and, suddenly, the island was visible through the fore part — a long, narrow strip of rock. a sandy beach on one side and steep cliff the other. Where the white surf broke against the headland, high up, three stunted palm trees grew close together.

Crispian saw no sign of Savage or his machines, and a feeling of uneasiness crept upon him.

'This could be a trap,' he warned the Karzians.

'Our screen is out,' came the prompt reply. 'He can do nothing.'

The island seemed harmless enough, but Crispian's apprehension increased as the spaceship dropped lower. If Savage were down there, he would not submit without a struggle . . .

'Savage doesn't have his screen up?' Mary asked abruptly

It was too quiet. Crispian's nerves were on edge — he had the feeling that something was wrong.

'No,' said the mechanical voice in answer to Mary's question, 'and he could not raise it now, without — '

At that moment, a blinding light flared up between the island and the ship. Crispian was dazzled and groped blindly for support as the spaceship shuddered along its entire length. So violent was the shock that he felt sure the ship was being torn apart. He was lifted in the air and thrown against the opposite wall — he experienced sharp pain and then there was numbness and darkness and nothing at all.

★ ★ ★

Savage watched from a safe distance as the two energy screens touched. After the flare-up, when the sea subsided, he saw that the island had gone. He stared at the empty sky, uncertain whether the space-ship had sunk beneath the waves or had been totally annihilated. In either case, he had nothing more to fear from the Karzians.

He laughed triumphantly. His plan to set off his screen by remote control, *inside* the range of the ship's screen, had succeeded perfectly. Two incompatible forces had reacted . . . and the result was in his favour. The Karzians were destroyed and Earth was his again to plunder.

From this second island, where he had set the trap, he stared around him. The sea was blue and glittering in the sunlight tall palms waved above him and the sand was a brilliant yellow and hot under his feet. It was all that a desert island should be, and yet — he was lonely for the human company he could not have. Mary would never be his, not now. It was too late for that.

He was trembling again, and sat down. This weakness was a new development and he knew what it meant; his end was near. The radiation to which he had been exposed at Stonehaven was taking its last and final effect. He was aware of physical changes in his body. It was not a pleasant way to die . . . his skin had begun to itch again and, in parts, was peeling away. Tufts of hair dropped out of his beard. The flesh of his fingers was becoming transparent, the bones showing through.

He lifted his hands to his face and stared at them, fascinated.

Not long now, ran the thought in his head. Not long to live. Not long to take his revenge on the world that had ruined him!

He roused himself by an effort and limped across the sand to where the alien machines hummed ceaselessly. He bent over them and caressed the spiral whorls as a lover caresses his beloved.

Insane laughter rocked his tortured body. He staggered, the sweat on his face giving him a wholly unhealthy aspect. He would not be beaten by physical weakness . . . not at the very moment success was at hand. He must hang on somehow.

He knew just what he was going to do and he laughed as he thought about it. He was going to wreck the whole planet!

21

Adrift in space

The stars were the first thing Crispian saw when he regained consciousness. His head ached as if someone beat a drum inside it and he thought it quite natural he should see stars. What puzzled him was the fact that they did not move.

They appeared as countless bright lights, mere pinpoints, entirely surrounded by blackness. It was a different kind of blackness to anything he had known before — as if it reached to eternity and were solid right through.

He remembered then, and tried to sit up, calling weakly:

'Mary!'

Gentle hands held his head and he sank back as pain shot through him.

'Lie still, darling,' Mary said softly. 'You took a nasty bump on the head. Just lie quietly till you feel better.'

He found her advice sensible, so he looked again at the stars.

'We're in space,' Mary informed him calmly. 'Somewhere outside the moon's orbit.'

In space, Crispian thought wildly, and turned his head. Through the port he saw a great shining disc — the moon, its surface pitted and scarred by meteoric craters. Beyond it, the Milky Way was a handful of glittering gems tossed on to black velvet. The sun blazed with naked incandescence directly ahead, the corona exposed in all its majesty.

He looked for Earth, and saw a tiny ball, almost colourless, the outlines of the oceans and continents scarcely visible; the sight gave him a sinking feeling. Would they ever get back, he wondered?

He forgot the pain in his head as he thought about their situation. The Karzians, he saw, were working furiously on a gigantic machine in the centre of the spaceship. He reached out to touch the translating machine, and asked:

'What's happening?'

The Karzians did not cease work to

answer. With hand-tools of the alien shell-shape, they concentrated on what they were doing.

'We are temporarily disabled. Savage operated his energy screen within range of our own, a contingency we had not anticipated. As soon as the two screens touched, there was an instant and violent repulsion. Savage's machine being anchored to Earth, we were hurled headlong into space.'

'Is the ship seriously damaged?' Crispian said, alarmed.

'Fortunately, the hull did not crack, so there is no immediate danger. Our engines were wrenched from their mountings, however, and until we can get the power connected again, we are helpless to control our flight. Already, we are accelerating under the sun's gravitational field.'

'You mean . . . falling into the sun?'

'Yes. We were flung beyond the effective reach of Earth's gravity, and the moon's pull is too weak to check us. Survival depends entirely on repairing the engines before it is too late.'

Crispian shuddered as he imagined their fate — falling through space into the heart of the sun, where incandescent gases reached a temperature of millions of degrees. He could feel the temperature inside the ship rising already.

'Is there anything we can do to help?' Mary asked.

'Nothing. It would be best if you were to lie down — gravitational pressure will increase as we approach the sun.'

'And we shan't be in the way,' Crispian murmured.

The increase in velocity became more noticeable as the moon dwindled in size. Earth lost its separate identity and merged into the background of stars. Venus showed, a crescent of light hanging in the black void.

Mary and Crispian sat on the metal floor with their backs against a curving wall. The fore porthole was filled with the glare of the sun until the Karzians dropped a filter over it. They sat and watched the luminous disc grow steadily larger.

'I wonder how long we've got?' Mary

said quietly. 'There must be a point of no-return. The orbit of Mercury, perhaps?'

Crispian nodded. Mercury was the planet nearest the sun; if the Karzians regained control of the ship in time, they could use Mercury's gravitational field to swing them away from the sun.

Mary said: 'I've no regrets, Arthur. If we must die, I'm glad we're together.'

He put his arm about her.

'I love you, Mary,' he said — and there was nothing more to say.

The hours passed and the temperature inside the spaceship rose as the pressure increased. Crispian removed his jacket, loosened his collar and slid into a horizontal position. The worst part was the waiting and knowing he could do nothing to help. He watched the Karzians at work — the feeling of tension grew.

The port directly overhead showed the black curtain of space and a sprinkling of stars; they seemed impossibly far away. By lifting his head he could look forward — the fiery disc of the sun almost filled the porthole and its flaming prominences reached out like grasping tentacles . . . it was not difficult to imagine them pulling the ship into its hungry maw. Occasionally, sunspots appeared as black dots on a luminous dial.

Pressure built up, clamping him to the floor and it became an effort to move at all. Sweat ran down his face and the metal hull burned under him. He would have given anything for a long, cooling drink of water.

The Karzians had ceased their croaking and now worked in silence. Crispian felt sorry for them, but at least they had something to do. He wondered how fast the ship was travelling; it would be accelerating all the time due to the effect of the sun's gravitational field.

There were moments when he lost consciousness, but always, when he opened his eyes, he saw the solid blackness of space above him. Earth, and Ralph Savage, seemed no longer real. There was only the ship, and the heat . . . and the threatening sun.

One time, he saw a small ring of light. Mercury. He tried to struggle upright, to shout a warning. They were passing Mercury — and the Karzians still failed to get the engines working.

This is it, Crispian thought. *The end. Death.* He looked at Mary lying beside him and death had the flavour of unfulfilled dreams.

★   ★   ★

'Well, professor,' said the Prime Minister. 'Can you offer any hope?'

Eurich blinked behind his spectacles.

'Not much, I'm afraid. I've perfected my detecting mechanism and can locate Savage any time — but that won't do us much good while he shelters behind an inter-atomic energy screen.'

'We've got to do something,' the Prime Minister returned. 'The position is critical. News from Greenwich is bad — the Karzian spaceship is still falling towards the sun, presumed out of control. It has passed beyond the orbit of Mercury and must be considered lost.'

Eurich nodded glumly. He had grown to like both Inspector Crispian and Mary

Marshall, and now he would never see them again. He felt a sense of loss.

'It's a tragedy,' he said.

But it was more than that. His grief was a personal thing — the loss of the spaceship meant that Savage was again master of the world.

'So we can expect no help from the Karzians — '

'None,' said the Prime Minister decisively. 'We are thrown back on our own resources — and the overall picture is not pleasant. The death of iron and steel means the complete breakdown of civilization; transportation has come practically to a standstill; our factories are idle from lack of power and raw materials. Starvation and mass-unemployment loom ahead — already there has been rioting in many cities. We are fighting for our existence and, unless Savage is stopped, I see no future for any of us.'

Eurich sighed heavily.

'And this new source of energy could have done so much good had it been used intelligently.'

'Quite so, professor, but that attitude is

somewhat unrealistic at the moment. We must rid ourselves of this madman . . . and, to that end, I propose forming a suicide squad, a band of men prepared to give their lives in reaching and killing Ralph Savage. These men will be placed at key points, ready for instant action and in direct communication with headquarters by a radio network. I want you to work in liaison with them. You will locate Savage — the rest is up to them.'

The Prime Minister paused, and angrily struck the table with his fist.

'Damn it,' he said irritably, 'there must be some moments when the screen is down and he is not in an inter-atomic state! We only need to get one man to him at such a time, and our worries are over.'

The professor rose to leave.

'I understand,' he said. 'I'll do what I can.'

* * *

Eurich's laboratory rapidly took on the air of a military H.Q. On a bench in the centre of the room was the detecting mechanism, a mass of tubes and wiring and indicator dials. In one corner was a small table where the commander of the suicide squad huddled over a radio transmitter; he was a sunburnt young man with a fierce moustache.

Opposite were camp beds and a supply of emergency rations. Outside the house, soldiers patrolled and a fast car stood ready if Eurich should need it. He himself left his detector only to snatch a few hours sleep, when an assistant took over his listening watch.

Every time Savage used a power beam, it was recorded on the professor's instruments — and Savage seemed to be making a lot of sorties from his hideout in the Pacific. So many, in fact, that Eurich became worried.

He muttered aloud: 'Mexico City — London — Cape Town! Why? Nothing happens at any of these places. I don't understand it.'

The army captain looked up from his radio.

'Reckon he's just making it more difficult for you, professor. Trying to throw you off the scent.'

But Eurich was not convinced. He worried the problem for days and, during that time, Savage operated in such distant places as India and China, Siberia and Scandinavia. He seemed to be making a world tour. He did not show himself and Eurich was completely at a loss to understand his movements.

At times, he would look up at the sky, towards the sun, and wonder about Crispian and Mary. It seemed impossible that they could still be alive — the spaceship was well past the orbit of Mercury and gathering momentum as it hurtled into the sun. And without the Karzians, Eurich did not think Earth stood much chance against Savage.

He returned to his immediate problem.

'Still based in the Pacific. Last movements above the Arctic Circle. Why? What the devil is he planning now?'

'Could be he ain't planning nothing,' the captain drawled. 'He hasn't done any more damage so far. My guess is that he's gone crazy and doesn't know what he's doing!'

Eurich shook his head. He was more worried than he cared to admit. He did not understand, but of one thing he felt sure — Savage was preparing some new and overwhelming disaster for the world.

22

Return to Earth

The sun was a blazing incandescence, filling the whole of the for'ard port; even with a filter over the port, the glare was intolerable. The air inside the spaceship was hot as a blast furnace, and the pressure due to acceleration built up as the ship rushed to destruction.

Crispian had awareness only for brief periods of time. Once, he heard Mary groan, but there was nothing he could do for her. His clothes were soaked with perspiration, and his limbs lead-heavy; he felt he was being slowly roasted to death.

A few of the Karzians still worked on the ship's engines — most of them lay unconscious on the floor, beaten by the terrible heat.

Crispian searched the black void behind them, looking among the jewel-like stars for the planet Mercury; it receded from him at alarming speed and there seemed no hope even if the Karzians succeeded in getting the motors to work again.

His small world was dominated by the vast bulk of the sun — a swirling mass of gases at millions of degrees Centigrade. And the ship fell headlong towards it. This was, he thought grimly, the nearest a man could get to Hell and still live . . .

He wondered about Savage and what was happening back on Earth, but it seemed too remote from the awful reality to matter.

The monstrous ball of fire directly ahead was the end of a nightmare. It would swallow them and hardly notice such a small mass . . . but he would be dead long before the ship itself was consumed.

He dozed again, thankful to have consciousness blotted out, and time passed.

When next he opened his eyes, he was aware of a subtle change. He could not account for it, but the heat had lessened and he found himself free of that crushing pressure. And seen through the fore part, the sun itself had become a ghostly, insubstantial thing.

He staggered upright and reached out to touch the translation machine. His throat was dry as dust and his words came out like the croak of a Karzian raven.

'What now?'

'Your ordeal is over,' the Karzians announced. 'There is nothing more to fear. We have completed the repairs and put the whole ship into the inter-atomic state. The sun no longer has any influence on us.'

'I don't feel any different,' Crispian said doubtfully.

'Naturally. That is because our condition is normal relative to the ship — but we and the ship are no longer part of the space-time continuum. Nothing material can affect us. It is a different application of the same system that enables us to travel faster than light.'

Mary had awakened, and she came over to him, smiling. She gripped his arm, and said:

'How small the sun looks!'

She pointed through the porthole, and the blazing orb that had threatened their lives was but a pale disc, strangely distant.

'We are returning to Earth immediately,' the Karzians informed them.

Mary said: 'And they mean, *immediately* — look!'

Directly ahead spun the blue-green globe of Earth, so close that Crispian could make out, through the cloudbanks, the contours of Europe and the English Channel.

He remembered what Savage had said. 'There is no time-factor involved in the inter-atomic state. Transmission is instantaneous.'

Even so, it was a shock to realize that the Karzians had already returned the ship to normal state and were slanting down to land.

He wondered, briefly: what sort of world would they find?

★   ★   ★

'Down periscope,' said the skipper briskly. 'Surface!'

The submarine glided up from the dark depths into the sunlit brilliance of the Pacific, and there was the target — Savage's island headquarters, unprotected for the moment by an energy screen.

'Look lively! Take a bearing, Number One. Gun crew stand by to fire!'

The First Lieutenant read off the bearing with practised ease. The gun-crew tensed, every man alert. They would not have a second chance . . .

For days the submarine had been standing off the island, submerged, and now the time for action had arrived. An atomic shell lay in the gun breech and, within seconds, Savage and the island would cease to exist.

If our luck holds, thought the skipper, and moistened his lips.

'Fire!'

But even as he spoke, a sheet of energy roared towards them. The submarine was engulfed, the atomic shell exploded in its breech and there was only vapour and a boiling sea. The suicide squad had been well-named.

Ralph Savage's lips curled into a sneer.

'The fools!' he muttered.

He steadied himself against the trunk of a tree as another attack of giddiness assailed him. His legs buckled under him and he slid, helpless, to the hot, yellow sand. Tears blurred the azure sky — tears of bitter frustration.

He cursed his failing strength. At the moment when he was ready to strike, to deliver his *coup de grâce*, he was in a state of near-collapse. His skin had a sallow pallor and his whole body was deteriorating from the effects of radioactivity — only his fanatical desire for revenge drove him on at all.

He lay with his back against a palm and drank a little wine to revive himself. He began to cough.

'The fools!' he said again.

His head swam, the trees danced before his eyes, and the lapping of waves against the reef was a soothing sound. Altogether too soothing . . . he roused himself. He must resist the temptation to sleep. Time, for him, was running out . . .

He struggled upright and swayed towards the alien machines. Their spiral forms seemed to come alive, writhing inexplicably, and he reached out his hands to them, stumbling, laughing insanely. His eyes burned with a feverish light.

Nothing could stop him now. Nothing. Earth would die with him

Professor Eurich stared appalled at the results of his calculations, his mind numbed by the enormity of Savage's scheme. For the first time, he understood what Savage's sorties meant — and it was the kind of knowledge he did not want.

He rose from his desk, opened the French windows and walked into the garden. An early morning mist shrouded the flowerbeds and the sun was but a vague redness trying to break through; he wondered if he would see another sunrise.

He looked long at the changing colour of the leaves, the effect of mist over the two elm trees at the far end of the garden, and sighed. It was a beautiful world — and now it was coming to an end.

He had to break the news — that was his job. He went indoors and called Downing Street on the phone. A secretary answered and he said:

'This is Professor Eurich. I am driving up immediately. Tell the Prime Minister that I have grave news for him.'

Then he went out to the car that stood waiting.

On the drive into London, he went over it in his mind for the hundredth time, but there was no way out that he could see. They would have to evacuate the cities and get as many people as possible on to high ground. A few might live through it to make a fresh start — a few score — a few hundreds, perhaps, of Earth's teeming millions.

He tried to imagine the panic that would ensue once his knowledge became generally known, and shuddered. Perhaps it would be better to keep quiet and say nothing? That was for the Prime Minister to decide. Eurich wanted only to forget.

The Prime Minister was waiting for him when he reached Downing Street, and the two men remained closeted together for more than an hour. When, finally, Eurich left, he felt as if a great weight had been lifted from his shoulders . . . the Prime Minister had decided to broadcast a warning to the whole world. After that, it would be every man for himself.

Professor Eurich returned to his garden to wait for the end; there, among the plants and flowers he had tended, he would spend his last hours. He felt too old to continue the struggle.

23

The World Wrecker

The Karzian spaceship circled Earth as it came in to land and, watching from a porthole, Crispian was puzzled by what he saw. It seemed to him that everyone had gone mad.

The cities were emptying, the roads thronged by refugees pushing barrows and carts of every description and loaded down by food and clothing and whatever household articles they could carry. And it was no isolated phenomenon. The same thing was happening right across the world; America, Asia, Africa — on small islands as well as large continents. There was a mass exodus, from the cities to the countryside, from the low lands to the hills.

'What the devil's going on down there?' Crispian muttered to himself.

He continued to watch as the ship

passed up the length of Italy. Rome was completely deserted, an incredible sight, and thousands of people straggled up the mountain paths of the Alps, dragging their precious possessions behind them; they looked like columns of ants on the march.

The plains of France were empty except for abandoned cattle, and smoke rose in a black spiral from the city of Brussels; to the north, the Dutch coast was the scene of furious activity as men worked ceaselessly to build the sea-walls to new and greater heights.

Across the Channel, where not one ship sailed, the roads out of London were choked with people leaving the capital. The South Downs, Leith Hill and Box Hill were black with crowds; the massed ranks of army tents and the large numbers of police indicated that the evacuation was officially controlled — yet the overall impression was still one of confusion and panic.

Mary said, bitterly, 'I suppose this is more of Savage's doing,' and turned expectantly towards the Karzians for an explanation.

But the giant ravens seemed just as baffled by what they saw.

'We shall land at once and find out what is happening,' the Karzians said through their translating machine. The silver ship plummeted through the clouds; the rockets fired briefly, and the ship was down. Salisbury Plain was deserted, and remained so; an air of brooding desolation hung over the great rocks of Stonehenge.

Crispian went outside and stared about him. The grassland stretched away to the distance and there was not a single person in sight.

'You'd think someone would come,' he said, 'if only out of curiosity. Well, I suppose we'll have to go looking on our own account — there must be somebody left who can tell us what this is about.'

Mary shivered.

'I don't like it,' she whispered. 'I don't like it at all.'

The Karzians addressed Crispian.

'If you are willing, we will place you in the inter-atomic state and transmit you to a group of your people. Then you can learn what the trouble is and inform us.'

'I'm willing,' he said crisply.

He was given a small, shell-like object to hold — remote control, Crispian thought, like Savage's black box.

'When you are ready to return,' the Karzians instructed him, 'grip the cone tightly — and we will do the rest.'

'Right — get on with it!' The Inspector had an after-thought. 'See if you can locate Professor Eurich; he's the man most likely to know the answer.'

'Very well. Now step close to the machine.'

Crispian waved to Mary and walked forward. The air hummed with power; he found himself without weight — and then the spaceship became insubstantial. The landscape shimmered like a wraith. Salisbury Plain vanished —

What followed next was a confused jumble of images; he was in a score of different places, almost simultaneously. He glimpsed deserted streets and silent laboratories, empty government offices. The scenes changed faster than he could identify them, as the Karzians transported him in search of Professor Eurich.

And then he was in a garden —

Eurich sat in a deckchair, relaxed; his eyes were closed and his expression peaceful.

Crispian called out: 'Hello, professor!'

At the sound of his voice, Eurich's eyes opened; he stared hard at Crispian, not believing what he saw, and his face lost colour. He rose to his feet, trembling.

'Inspector — you! It's not possible . . . you're dead. The spaceship fell into the sun — '

Crispian laughed, and let his hand fall on to the professor's shoulder.

'Not quite,' he said, 'but damn near it. Anyway, I'm back among the living . . . and now, what is going on here? London's empty and — '

Eurich gripped Crispian's hands and looked searchingly into his eyes.

'You're all right? And Mary?'

'Yes. She's with the ship, on Salisbury Plain.'

'The Karzians are back?' Eurich demanded eagerly.

'Yes, we — '

'Thank God for it, for they alone can

save us! Savage will destroy us all unless we act quickly . . . you must take me to the Karzians at once. There is little enough time to do anything.'

Crispian thought fast. It had worked once; it should work again.

'All right, professor. Keep close to me.'

He pressed the shell-shaped cone . . .

★ ★ ★

They were standing on Salisbury Plain, and there was the spaceship, a silver column towering above them, and the Karzians, black wings folded, waiting, and Mary. Eurich wasted no time; he ran towards the translator, rested one hand on it, and spoke rapidly.

'Savage plans to destroy the whole world,' he said. 'He has placed a piece of rock — in the inter-atomic state — under every capital and major city across the planet. The rocks are there — now! And he can change them all back to normal matter simultaneously . . . imagine it, more than fifty earthquakes such as Lima suffered, at one moment. The crust of the planet is liable to crack completely!'

Crispian swore, understanding the mass evacuations he had witnessed. Away from the cities, but —

Eurich had not finished.

'That isn't all. He has placed similar rocks under the Arctic and Antarctic ice. When these revert to normal, the heat generated will melt the ice floes and the level of the oceans will rise sharply. All low-lying country will be flooded . . . '

Away from the cities — and into the mountains! It was explained now. Savage's scheme was revealed in all its horror.

Millions of people would die; Earth would be wrecked by upheavals and tidal waves on a scale unimaginable.

Mary turned pale.

'The devil!' she said.

Eurich appealed to the Karzians: 'Can you do anything to stop him?'

'We must act quickly,' the giant ravens replied. 'We will locate each rock-fragment and remove it, but that will take time and Savage must not be allowed to act. We must deal with him immediately.

Inspector Crispian, are you willing to enter the inter-atomic state again?'

'I'll do whatever you consider necessary,' Crispian said.

'Good. The point is that Savage's only way of escape is into the inter-atomic world — we must drive him there and keep him on the run. You will, of course, both be solid relative to each other, though the world about you will appear insubstantial. You must keep after him until you have rendered him helpless. Do you understand?'

'Sure,' Crispian said. 'But exactly how do I find him in the inter-atomic world? If we're both moving through solid obstacles — '

'Leave that to us. We shall direct you.'

'Right,' Crispian said briskly.

Mary touched his arm, smiling faintly.

'Be careful, Arthur,' she whispered. 'I don't want to lose you now.'

'I'll be careful,' he promised, and kissed her.

Then, still gripping the shell-like cone, he stepped once more up to the Karzian transmitter. To those watching, he became ethereal, and vanished altogether.

'Now we will deal with the threat to your cities,' the Karzians said calmly.

Mary and Professor Eurich entered the spaceship; the port closed and it rose into the air. Cruising high above the clouds, the Karzians set about tracing the danger points under Earth's cities and ice fields.

Eurich wondered . . . could the Karzians save the world before Savage completely destroyed it?

★ ★ ★

Crispian stood on a sandy beach — more accurately, hovered in the air a few inches above it. Ghostly palms swayed in a breeze he could not feel and blue water lapped soundlessly against the reef. The sun was a faint halo high above him, but he had no sensation of heat. This was the first time he had been long enough in the interatomic state to have any feeling about it, and he studied his reactions with interest.

Further along the beach, Ralph Savage bent over his machines. He was not yet aware of the Inspector's approach.

Crispian moved forward, his feet touching nothing solid. It was a curious sensation, like swimming in air, unnerving till he got used to the idea. A tree grew directly in his path. He passed through it, feeling nothing, as if it were only a mirage.

Just then, Savage turned — and for both men it was a shock. Savage believed Crispian dead; it was incredible that the Inspector should be here. His lips drew back in a snarl and he cursed.

Crispian saw how much the scientist had changed; his beard had gone and his skin was dead-white, almost transparent. It was obvious that Savage was dying — only the intense brightness of his eyes revealed the temper of the man, the terrible power of his need for revenge that drove him on.

Crispian moved forward quickly.

Savage hesitated. It needed only seconds for him to complete his work; but Crispian was upon him. He touched the black box at his waist and disappeared.

Crispian regarded an empty beach.

Where was Savage now? He pressed his cone, and so began the most fantastic chase of all time.

★ ★ ★

Aboard the Karzian ship, Mary and Professor Eurich found themselves virtually ignored. The giant ravens tended their machines with an air of purpose; the whole ship vibrated with power.

Eurich had started to take notes of everything he saw on the spaceship, but his heart was not in it. On the planet below, millions of people were in the gravest danger — and he doubted even the Karzians' ability to avert disaster now.

Mary's thoughts were with Crispian; she dreaded that something might happen to the man she loved; but at least that kept her mind off the holocaust that would follow if Savage succeeded in his plan. It would be Lima all over again, magnified fifty times . . . perhaps the Earth's crust would completely shatter under such violent stress.

They waited for news and, presently,

the Karzians spoke:

'We have located all the rock fragments and have begun their removal. It is not a simple matter, and will take time, for we can only deal with one piece of inter-atomic rock at a time. We need to fix a beam of inter-atomic energy on each rock-fragment, transmit it to a safe place, and there return it to normal matter. The success of the operation depends entirely on keeping Savage occupied till we have completed our work.'

But if Savage strikes first, Mary thought . . .

'Where is he now?' she asked tensely.

There was a pause.

'The plan to divert Savage's attention proceeds well. Inspector Crispian's sudden appearance shocked him into leaving the island — and he must return to the machines before he can execute his plan. The Inspector is giving chase. It remains only to keep him on the run . . . then we can concentrate on Savage himself.'

Time passed slowly aboard the space-ship, each second threatening to bring disaster. On Earth, the hillsides echoed to the chanting of mass prayers. In some places there was fighting, and many fell to their death from high places.

The whole world waited for catastrophe.

24

World of Ghosts

Crispian was somewhere under the Pacific. Blue-green water swirled about him, and the light filtering down from above was as vari-coloured as though the sun shone through a stained-glass window. The sand bank sloped gently into the depths, broken here and there by coral formations or masses of floating weed. Occasionally a shining fish investigated him, then turned away with a flick of its tail.

Savage was a dim figure ahead of him in the water. The Karzians kept track of his quarry and directed his pursuit.

The land-shelf ended abruptly, and there was a sharp drop. He floated down, wondering how it was he could still breathe, and assumed it was because time did not exist in his present inter-atomic state. His lungs, already filled with air, would enable him to survive until he returned to the normal world. He experienced no sensation of wetness and his clothes did not hamper him in any way.

From time to time, Savage looked over his shoulder; he kept moving on. Once an octopus surprised him, and tried to seize him in its tentacles — he drifted through them as though they did not exist.

Crispian marvelled at the beauty of the underwater world around him, and realized what a superb technique the Karzians had evolved for exploring otherwise inaccessible places. He was in a world of ghosts; moving through the interstices between atoms of matter. It gave him an exhilarating sense of freedom.

Savage was slowing down, tiring — and, as Crispian gained on him, touched the black box and vanished again.

★ ★ ★

The Karzians made their first report:

'Both ice caps are safe. The pieces of inter-atomic rock have been removed from beneath the Arctic and Antarctic.

Your world is now safe from flooding . . . '

For Mary, it was the first time she fully realized that a choice must be made; that some cities might be saved at the expense of others. She was glad she did not have to choose — and hoped that London would be high on the list.

Eurich nodded. The Karzians had been wise in dealing with the ice caps first. Now, no matter what happened, there would be no danger from millions of tons of water rushing to drown survivors. But unless they could prevent the majority of threatened earthquakes, the outer crust of the planet might still buckle and —

He could not grasp the full implications of that.

★ ★ ★

Crispian was still under water, but the darkness indicated that he was at a greater depth than before. A forest of weeds grew all about him, and he caught glimpses of the strange creatures that lived far down in the ocean. Savage must be nearby, somewhere . . .

He strained his eyes to pierce the gloom. Great blocks of stone lay tumbled about, worn smooth by the gentle motion of the sea and covered by weeds and molluscs. A stone caryatid thrust solemnly upwards. He traversed a tesellated pavement and saw the ruins of great archways — here, under the waves, he viewed all that was left of some prehistoric civilization.

Fish swam in and out of the sunken city, their cold eyes watchful for the intruder. The eeriness of the place got on his nerves. He began to *feel* like a ghost . . . panic touched him with her icy fingers. He wanted only to return to the world of sunlight and sanity.

Other eyes glittered beyond the next stone column — Ralph Savage!

Crispian went forward again. He must keep after Savage, never giving him a moment to stop and think, keep after him till the Karzians had removed the last threat to Earth's cities. Suddenly, Savage disappeared.

The mechanical voice of the translating machine boomed out:

'London is safe. And Paris. We are operating next under New York . . . '

Mary gave a sigh of relief. It was illogical, she knew, the safety of London was illusory when at any moment Earth itself might split asunder, but still she felt relief because the immediate danger to the capital had been removed.

Eurich was calculating chances. How many cities could they afford to lose? Savage's weapon was more powerful than any hydrogen bomb and the explosion took place under the Earth's crust. There was a long way to go yet before he could relax.

★ ★ ★

Crispian was dazzled by a blue-white glitter. The snowfields stretched interminably to a wall of ice that rose sheer to the sky. He was surprised he had no sense of cold. Away to his left, the ice floes moved — giant bergs forcing a passage to the sea. There was a breath-taking grandeur in the scene.

The snow started with a small flurry, shrouding the figure of Savage in white. The intense glare of the ice worried him; and the snow came faster, blotting out all but that huge white wall and the dark figure at its base. He kept moving towards it.

The silence was terrifying. He was alone in a translucent world, cut off forever. Nothing existed except the giant bergs and the driving snow and his quarry. The chase developed a dreamlike quality.

He moved through a wasteland under a harsh blue-white light, with the falling snow like some phantom wall before him. The glass-smooth walls of a crevasse dropped away at his feet ... Savage looked back. His hand moved to his waist — and he was gone again.

★ ★ ★

The Karzians said: 'New York is safe, and Los Angeles, and Mexico City ... '

Los Angeles. Mary gasped. Somehow she hadn't thought of that fantastic metropolis of film and television and beauty contests as being in danger. It had seemed a modern fairyland, remote from reality . . . but now, like any other city, the streets would be empty and silent.

Professor Eurich crossed off names on a list — and counted those that remained. His lips compressed. The odds were still in Savage's favour. Although not a deeply religious man, he offered up a prayer.

'The Inspector is doing well,' the Karzians continued. 'He keeps Savage hard-pressed and gains on him all the time.'

Mary clenched her hands. What was it like, she wondered, roaming the world without material substance, a living ghost?

★　★　★

Now he was deep underground, penetrating the impenetrable. The darkness was solid as the rock through which he passed, effortlessly, like a blind man falling through the sky. He had no idea where Savage was, and relied on the

Karzians to guide him.

The rock opened out, and a faint glimmer of light showed the ochre-streaked walls of a mighty cavern. A torrent of water rushed through it and disappeared down a black tunnel at the lower end. Crispian saw Savage moving upstream, and followed him under the flickering curtain of a waterfall. There was darkness again.

Beyond was a series of small grottoes where stalactites, brilliantly coloured, hung from the roof and strange rock formations stood like frozen statues in the gloom. Savage descended into a chasm. How far below the surface were they now, Crispian wondered? The abyss ended and the chase continued through more caves.

In one place, prehistoric man had left his mark on the walls, but Crispian dared not stop to look. He hurried along a narrow gallery, half-filled with water, and passed a fall of rock. He was close enough to Savage to see the sweat on his face, to read in his expression the desperation of a dying man, almost near enough to take him —

'Berlin and Rome and Moscow . . . '

Eurich crossed off more names. The balance was swinging. There was hope now.

Mary stared at the giant birds and wondered if they could protect Crispian if he should need it.

'Arthur,' she whispered. 'Arthur, come back to me!'

★ ★ ★

The city was oriental, there could be no doubt of that. And it was deserted, grim reminder of the threat hanging over the world. Crispian moved through a hall where the glitter of gilt and blaze of colour almost overwhelmed him. He came to a courtyard with high walls and grilles over the windows.

Savage vanished into a wall and Crispian followed him. A magnificent banquet lay untouched on the long table. He passed through exotic rooms where discarded clothing told of hasty flight.

Savage turned, lips drawn back in a snarl, and Crispian reached out . . .

The tempo increased. Now he was skimming through the air . . . now flitting through empty buildings . . . now it was a jungle. Savage was tiring, unable to shake off his pursuer. He touched the black box once more.

★ ★ ★

Crispian experienced again the darkness of solid rock. He moved warily, knowing the end was at hand. Savage must turn and fight, and he had the advantage of surprise — he could pick the time and place for his attack.

It must come soon. Savage would try to kill him so that he could return to the island and use the alien machines. He wondered how far the Karzians had got with negating the menace to Earth's cities . . .

Crispian saw a tunnel lit by a dull red glow and Savage just ahead of him. The redness grew in intensity, casting sinister shadows over the bare walls; the tunnel opened out, sloping down to a funnel-shaped crater. Savage reached the end of the passage and leapt into the void —

Crispian jumped too, close behind — and shut his eyes as he saw what lay below. Savage had led him to the fiery heart of a volcano and he was falling towards a cauldron where molten lava bubbled and lurid flames danced. It was like a scene from a painting by Bosch.

It can't hurt you, he screamed soundlessly at himself. Then a sharp blow in his groin brought him back to a sense of his real danger — Savage had chosen this moment to attack him.

He opened his eyes and struck back, feeling a peculiar satisfaction as his fists hammered solid flesh. It had been so long since he felt anything solid. Savage twisted like an eel and got behind him — he felt a knee dig viciously into the small of his back and a sinewy arm caught him under the chin, forcing his head back.

Crispian used all his strength to break free and rebounded violently . . . he sank into molten rock, and crimson flames flicked eerily in his face. There was no sensation of heat, no suffocation, only an angry redness.

Savage dived after him and they locked again in combat. Savage had lost his advantage and was mortally sick, but still he fought with the strength of a madman. They struggled desperately in the red hellfire of volcanic magma, and still there was doubt as to who would be the victor.

Savage had him by the throat, his mouth moving in soundless curses, hatred blazing in his eyes. Crispian caught at a brittle finger and wrenched, breaking it. He wriggled free and slugged heavy blows at Savage's heart, and saw him wince.

The rock boiled around them. Savage made one last effort to finish Crispian, failed, and sought to escape — but before he could touch the black box at his waist, Crispian seized his wrists and clamped them together. He swung a punch at Savage's jaw and, suddenly, it was over.

He held the unconscious body close to him and pressed the cone for return.

25

Aftermath

It was fine to feel the solid deck of the spaceship under him again, and see Mary running towards him. He let Savage slide to the floor and held out his arms for her.

She hugged him, crying: 'It's finished, Arthur. The Karzians have removed every piece of rock from under the ground and Earth is safe again!'

Professor Eurich bent over Savage and examined him.

'I doubt if he will regain consciousness — he's too far gone.'

But the giant ravens from Karz had their own methods. The body of Savage was lifted and placed inside one of their machines.

'He will live,' they assured the professor. 'We shall take him back with us. You must report his death to your governments, for he will not trouble you again.'

'He could have been a great man,' Eurich said wistfully, 'if his mind hadn't warped.'

'He still can be,' the Karzians replied. 'One day, you will understand . . . '

Crispian released Mary; he still found it hard to believe that the danger was past.

'What about Savage's machines?' he asked. 'They can't be left where they are.'

'We are going to collect them, then we shall return you to your own country before we leave for Karz. The machines will go with us.'

'Won't you consider staying?' the professor broke in. 'There is so much we could learn from you.'

'No. We have interfered enough, and your race has far to go before it can meet another on terms of equality. We shall be waiting. One day it will happen — till then, it is better for us not to meet.'

There was a pause. The bright eyes of the Karzians regarded them steadily, and the voice from the translator said:

'This is goodbye.'

★ ★ ★

Crispian stood on Salisbury Plain and the silver spaceship pointed its nose to the sky, ready for takeoff. The final parting was about to take place, without ceremony. Earth had been saved and now the Karzians were going home . . .

He was a little sad at the thought, for he had come to respect the giant ravens, and his feeling showed in his face. Mary, beside him, slipped her hand into his; he gripped it hard.

Eurich moved about restlessly, and said, for the hundredth time: 'They shouldn't be leaving like this — we haven't thanked them properly.'

There was a long silence before the rockets fired and the ship rose like a silver bullet, jets stabbing red flame. It rapidly became a tiny speck in the sky, and then disappeared from sight.

Mary uttered a sigh of relief.

'Well, that's over,' she said in a practical tone of voice. 'I'm glad they've gone. I suppose they were all right in their way, but their way is not ours. We have to live our own lives.'

Eurich shook his head gloomily.

'A great loss to science,' he muttered. 'An incalculable loss.'

Crispian threw off his feeling of regret. Mary was right — the human race had to make its own way and its own mistakes. There were no short cuts to evolution.

'Never mind, professor — you still have your notes. You'll work it all out and end up ahead of the Karzians yet . . . anyway, if it consoles you at all, you can be best man at our wedding!'

★　★　★

The Karzian story lasted exactly one week on the front pages of the world's newspapers; then it was relegated to an inside column; and from there to an occasional tailpiece. It seemed that most of humanity was only too glad to forget the Karzians had ever visited Earth.

The cities began to fill up, the wheels of industry turned again and civilization got back in its stride. The menace of Ralph Savage was forgotten when iron and steel could once more be manufactured. Transport came to life and food and raw materials flowed freely across the planet . . . only a few visionaries, Professor Eurich among them, planned for the day when a ship of Earth would cross the void of interstellar space, to Karz!

Meanwhile, Crispian and Mary had married and set up home together. In their new happiness, they soon forgot the dangers they had been through, and it was only for a moment, looking up at the night sky, that Crispian wondered:

What was happening to Ralph Savage on Karz?

Epilogue

He did not remember very much.

He lay on his back, on fine red dust, and looked at the carved arabesques above him. Then he rolled over and sat up; through an opening in the wall, he saw the sand dunes, rust-red and streaked with ochre. Where am I, he wondered? *Who am I?*

He rose and stretched himself, feeling wonderfully alive. He breathed deep of an air carrying unfamiliar scents, and flexed his muscles. A brightly polished circle of metal reflected his image; he saw a tall, young man with long, dark hair, his face unmarked — a handsome face. He felt good, as if all the poisons had been drained from his body and new energy poured into it. He wanted to run and leap about.

Dark memories shifted at the back of his mind, but they were lost before full realization came.

He went outside. The sky was a lovely, pastel blue, and the sweeping vista of sand reached unbroken to the horizon. Behind him, the building he had just left was like something out of wonderland, red coral fashioned in the shape of a sea-shell.

He walked a little way beyond the building, to where the sand ended, and looked down into a vee-shaped chasm. Water sparkled in the sunlight, crystal clear.

There was a whirr of wings overhead, and the birds descended. Huge, black birds with heavy bills and irridescent feathers. He clapped his hands delightedly as one of the birds landed beside him.

'How do you feel now?' the bird asked politely.

He did not think it strange for a bird to speak his own language.

'Wonderful,' he answered with enthusiasm. 'I can't remember ever feeling so good. In fact, I can't remember — '

'That is well,' the bird said. 'There is much for you to do here. You will be instructed in the science of inter-atomic energy and, later, will join a research team. We welcome the addition of a new mind — a new type of mind — to our problems. You will play an important part in developing the resources of our planet.'

'I don't know —' he began, and stopped. What had he been about to say? His brow wrinkled, for the thought eluded him completely.

The bird watched him closely with its bright eyes.

'You will always have difficulty in remembering the past,' it told him. 'But you must not worry about that. It should be enough that you have work to do.' The bird paused. 'Your own people would have killed you . . . we saved you. You are one of us now.'

'I'm grateful,' he said.

'We had to adapt your lungs to breathe our atmosphere. We healed your body and your mind. The work that you will do here will one day benefit your own people — is that sufficient?'

'I'm grateful,' he repeated.

'Very well. Don't try to remember the

past, for that could only bring sadness and regret. The future is yours to do with as you will. Your instruction will commence now . . . '

★ ★ ★

In the days that followed, he adapted quickly to his new life and found complete satisfaction in his work. He began to take it for granted that he was the only one of his kind, and that the birds were by far his mental superiors.

His life was a simple one. He was given food and shelter and, in return, he worked. The birds had a social life of their own, but the form it took was alien to him and he could not join in. He was an outcast; for him, there was only work and sleep.

Scientific research was always harnessed to practical problems. The planet was ageing, a vast dust bowl with a dwindling water supply; canals silted up and the scanty vegetation died. There was a continuous struggle to survive, to force a living from the land.

The atmosphere, too, was escaping into space — a slow but relentless process. Unless the birds solved all these problems, they would one day have to take their ships and go looking for a new home. So Savage worked hard, for this was his home too, and he did not want to leave.

It was only at night, when the long twilight closed in and he stood under the triple moons, that he searched for the faintly twinkling star of Sol; in those moments, there was a strange longing inside him — and, sometimes, tears in his eyes.

THE END

We do hope that you have enjoyed reading this large print book.

Did you know that all of our titles are available for purchase?

We publish a wide range of high quality large print books including:
Romances, Mysteries, Classics
General Fiction
Non Fiction and Westerns

Special interest titles available in large print are:
The Little Oxford Dictionary
Music Book, Song Book
Hymn Book, Service Book

Also available from us courtesy of Oxford University Press:
Young Readers' Dictionary
(large print edition)
Young Readers' Thesaurus
(large print edition)

For further information or a free brochure, please contact us at:
Ulverscroft Large Print Books Ltd.,
The Green, Bradgate Road, Anstey,
Leicester, LE7 7FU, England.
Tel: (00 44) **0116 236 4325**
Fax: (00 44) **0116 234 0205**

THE RESURRECTED MAN

E. C. Tubb

After abandoning his ship, space pilot Captain Baron dies in space, his body frozen and perfectly preserved. Five years later, doctors Le Maitre and Whitney, restore him to life using an experimental surgical technique. However, returning to Earth, Baron realises that now being legally dead, his only asset is the novelty of being a Resurrected Man. And, being ruthlessly exploited as such, he commits murder — but Inspector McMillan and his team discover that Baron is no longer quite human . . .

THE UNDEAD

John Glasby

On the lonely moor stood five ancient headstones, where a church pointed a spectral finger at the sky. There were those who'd been buried there for three centuries, people who had mingled with inexplicable things of the Dark. People like the de Ruys family, the last of whom had died three hundred years ago leaving the manor house deserted. Until Angela de Ruys came from America, claiming to be a descendant of the old family. Then the horror began . . .

CARLA'S REVENGE

Sydney J. Bounds

Society girl Carla Bowman is young, beautiful — and wild. She is the honey of King Logan, a gangster running a protection racket on New York's East Side, and she becomes caught up in violence and bloodshed. Carla double-crosses Logan and joins his rival, Sylvester Shapirro, only to become his captive in a sanatorium. She escapes, but when she learns that Shapirro has killed her father, Carla's only desire is to revenge her father's death — whatever the cost to herself . . .